CH00835673

GONE TOMORROW

NILZA ELITA

For information contact: www.nilzaelita.com
Edited by - Miranda Summers-Pritchard
TITLE Copyright © 2019 by Nilza Elita.

This book is dedicated to Sasha, Jay and Vasco, for believing in me. I love you all so much.

And also to: Agatha Christie: The Queen of Crime. If I am half the writer you were, I consider myself fortunate.
If hadn't loved your work since I first started to read crime, then I would't be the writer I am today.
You paved the way for me to follow.
Thank you so much.

E verything happens in threes. But this time, what happened was death.

'Three deaths in one month, how am I going to get through this? It's unbelievable!' Rebecca muttered to herself.

'What did you say, darling?' Her mother asked.

'Nothing.' She looked away, trying not to cry.

They were at her grandmother's funeral, Rebecca knew her grandmother was old but with Lara and Macy both dead too, it was just too much.

The funeral of Rebecca's paternal grandmother was nearly over. She had died in her sleep four days ago, and the family were grateful she that had gone peacefully.

Recently though, Rebecca had found out her childhood friend Lara, whom she saw once or twice a year, had committed suicide two weeks ago. She hadn't attended her funeral because she'd only found out about her death the day after her grandmother died and by then, the cremation had already taken place.

Rebecca had only just met Lara a month ago for a lunch date, that's what bugged her the most. Lara had cancelled a previous meeting with her because she was due to start her dream job at a top city company, working in HR. So, they had agreed to meet after she had started her job, that way she could tell Rebecca all about it when they met.

They eventually had their postponed lunch date – last month. Lara had gushed about her new job, colleagues and how she could now afford to move out of her parents' house and buy a starter home with her boyfriend. She suspected he was about to propose to her, which had got her even more excited. The two girls had eagerly looked on Instagram for engagement ring designs they liked.

'It's all speculation for now, Bec, but he is so devoted to me — that's why I sense he will get down on one knee any day now.' She threw her head back and laughed.

Lara, Rebecca's boyfriend Matt and some of her friends called her Bec. Finn Reid, her dad, called her Frey on account of the thousands of freckles on her face.

Everything had been going well for Lara when they'd met last month, what had possessed her to her kill herself? Rebecca was so confused.

Normally, that would have been bad enough but there was another funeral she had to attend to that week, which would be even more difficult: her boyfriend's mother, Macy Rook, had died outside her house ten days ago. The police said they'd found her under a bush in her front garden with 'multiple stab wounds'. Despite medical attention at the scene, she had died on the way to the hospital.

It was all a mess, just over two weeks and three people she knew had gone. They always say things come in threes!

Rebecca sat next to her mother at the wake, her mind a million miles away. Her father was not saying much considering his mother had died. He didn't cry during the service, he held his composure. Rebecca's mother, Erin Reid, in comparison, nattered away as if they at a party. She looked at her mother, who, if she removed her hat, was dressed like she was going for a Christmas night out. She wore a black, tight-fitting one-shoulder dress that had a big bow on the sleeve. Her hair had been immaculately blow-dried by the hairdressers that morning, and she had adorned her head with a big black fashionable hat. To Rebecca, it looked like a black dinner plate placed slightly off centre with a plume of black feathers jutting out. Her hair still looked like not a strand was out of place. She'd had her nails done the day before in a nude colour. She had shown Rebecca her nails when she'd got back from the salon,

'Look at my nails, aren't they nice and subtle for the funeral?' Rebecca agreed and hoped that she would blend into the crowd the next day.

But here she sat, with the least subtle funeral outfit, hair, make-up and sparkly black clutch bag, but her nails were fine! Rebecca shrugged, there was no point saying anything to her, her mother did whatever she liked and there was nothing she or her father could say that could make a difference.

'Come on, the food is out. Let's eat, I'm starving.' Erin said, nudging her daughter.

'Mum, for God's sake! Why don't you help dad out, instead of sitting here spectator!' She flashed a stare at her mother, keeping her voice low, so nobody could hear her.

'Stop fretting – he's got the caterers to help him. Don't get annoyed at me – you're young, you don't know what funerals are like. They are so boring, and it's a chore being here.'

'Young? I am twenty-six, not a baby, Mum!' She gave a big sigh, and she marched towards her father, but her annoyance at her mother's devil-may-care attitude dissipated as soon she looked at him. He truly was suffering in silence.

'Dad, how are you holding up? Don't worry, it will all be over soon, I love you dad, we will get through this.' She offered him a sympathetic smile.

'I know, Frey,' he said, looking down at her with a dour expression, rubbing his forehead at the same time.

He then caressed her masses of red hair trying to soothe her.

Watching her father go to talk to someone else, she scanned the room and saw her boyfriend Matt, at the far end of the room. She smoothed her black pencil skirt, made sure she tucked her silk blouse into her skirt and walked over to him.

Matt was struggling to come to terms with his mother's death and she didn't have the words to console him. She tried her best, but lately, he had become like a zombie. His mother was all he'd had, his dad had died when he was young. Rebecca had only met her twice, but, she was heartbroken seeing Matt like this. And for his mother to die in that way, it was something that happened to other people, not someone they knew!

Her parents supported Matt too, her dad cooked him food and they invited him over for meals at their house, but Matt was just going through the motions and not talking. When he did speak to Rebecca, it was to say he wanted to be alone. His aunt, uncle and close family friends made the funeral arrangements and Matt accepted what they decided like an automaton.

Rebecca remembered how much fun they'd had together during their relationship over the last few years. Matt could make her laugh and if something troubled her, he always said, 'Bec, you are my beautiful, sexy girlfriend – with that red hair of yours, nobody would mess with you – you know what they say about redheads!' Just saying silly things like that made her smile, even if she didn't want to.

Matt told her he loved watching her sleep because she looked so perfect. He put her on an invisible pedestal and admired her from there. Secretly, Rebecca loved the attention she got from him, although sometimes she felt it was a bit much. But now, whilst he was dealing with the death of his mother, she was feeling as if she was being shut out by him, but she understood she had to give him space and time.

Rebecca vented her frustrations about Matt to her father. Finn suggested just being there for him. Even if he said nothing to her, just being close to him would do. Although Rebecca wished she could do more, she knew her dad was right, she had to be patient.

Now, here at the funeral of her grandmother, she was trying to console her dad. She prayed for a normal day again.

A few days after the funeral, she'd had the most amazing dream, she was flying through the clouds giggling. It was like being on a rollercoaster - up and down, up and down she flew. It was exhilarating, she was having fun, she was happy.

Her alarm woke her from the dream, she looked at her phone to switch it off. She was still smiling, but then the smile died on her lips as she remembered the gloom of the past few weeks. She was due to visit Lara's parents to give her condolences today, and she wasn't sure how it would go. Erin said she would take her there – Erin had liked Lara too. That was a relief, she didn't want to go alone. She needed to show her support and love of Lara and let her parents know how much Lara had meant to her. She had to stay strong for their sake – she told herself not to cry in front of them.

Rebecca opened her cupboard to take out the black silk blouse she'd bought for her gran's funeral and her black jeans. She put the blouse on, tucking it into her jeans and glimpsed in the mirror to check it looked right. Yes, that would do, the jeans made it informal. She fished her flat black pumps from her wardrobe then went downstairs to have breakfast.

Her appearance would be the last thing on Lara's parents' mind. When Rebecca reached the kitchen, she found that her father had already gone to work. Her mother wasn't around – she guessed she was still in her room getting ready, so she made toast and tea whilst she waited for her, her mind was lost in thought about Matt. She had sent him a quick 'Good Morning' text when she'd woken as she always did.

Now, sitting here waiting for the kettle to boil, she sent him another one,

'How did you sleep last night, my baby? I am ready to meet with Lara's parents this morning, my mum is driving me there. Remember, I told you I was going there today? Hope to catch you later. I will come over after lunch. I love you. xxx'

7

Matt was answering her messages sporadically these days, almost as if he was not by his phone for hours, then seeing her message and replying back. Rebecca noticed he was spending more time staring at the TV, not paying attention to any programme in particular. It was sad to watch, but she understood his behaviour. Macy's funeral was next.

The police couldn't make sense of Macy's murder. They suspected it was someone who was on drugs, demanding money, and when Macy didn't give it or maybe had none on her, they'd stabbed her and stolen her bag and phone. Her car was untouched, the keys were still on her when she was found, but her handbag and phone were missing. The police had investigated the matter, but from what Rebecca could gather they had nothing concrete to go on. If it had been a random stabbing for money, their hopes of finding a killer were slim and with the police cuts in funding, there was little hope that the investigation would carry on for much longer.

They scheduled the funeral for three days' time. They would release Macy's body to the family to put her to rest. The police had all the forensic information they needed. Rebecca assumed it would just be another unsolved murder to add to the hundreds on their list. A senseless killing for money – Macy had only been in her mid-forties.

'Darling you're eating breakfast already? Why didn't you wait for me?' Erin asked.

Rebecca looked up startled, she must have been so

deep in thought she hadn't heard her mother come downstairs. She was wearing a black jumpsuit and headband to give her hair a tidy appearance. This was typical of Erin, she liked to make a splash regardless of the occasion, or non-occasion in this case. As usual, she said nothing to her mother about her attire. It would be pointless, she never listened to her anyway.

'I wasn't sure how long you'd be and I was hungry.'

'How are you feeling about today darling? You chose something plain and simple, not extravagant like me!' she said, laughing.

Erin was a good-looking woman in her late forties with fiery red hair which she kept long. Her green eyes supported lashes that many women would pay a lot of money for. Her friends were envious of them because they were long and thick. She was just over five feet tall, slim and petite. She believed high heels were a necessity.

Although she tried to be a good mother to her only daughter Rebecca, she wasn't very 'mumsy'. Rebecca didn't notice the difference at first, but her dad knew Erin came across as unfeeling sometimes, but he would never explain why she was this way. He said she was different, then quickly changed the subject.

Erin had married Finn when she was twenty-two, she had given birth to Rebecca at twenty-four and wanted no more children. She never again wanted to be big, fat and horrible like she had been whilst pregnant with Rebecca! It had been a nightmare, she had lost her figure, her skin had become blotchy and she couldn't eat her favourite foods because they had to be fully cooked. So, she'd had to give up smoked salmon and have her steaks well done instead of medium rare the way she liked it. Her eggs too, had needed to be thoroughly cooked and she stopped drinking wine, her weekend drink of choice.

Rebecca always wondered why given Erin's background, her parents never mentioned her Scottish relatives or even friends – her mother clammed up whenever she asked. She also remembered the slap she received when she was around ten years old. Once, Rebecca overheard her parents arguing with Erin's sister who had come down for a surprise visit. Erin had shut the door in her face and Finn had had to apologise to an aunt she didn't even know she had until then!

They never heard from her again. When Rebecca had asked her mother why she wouldn't see her, Erin had given her a hard slap and sent her to her room. Finn tried to console her, telling her that her mother was unwell, but it took her a long time to forgive her mother. It was a simple question, now, as a grown-up, she wanted to reconnect with her Scottish family, but she still dared not ask her mother about it. She considered asking her father, but knew she had to wait while he was still dealing with grief. She didn't want to complicate matters with her parents at the moment.

Now, in the kitchen, she told Erin, 'At least you admit you overdo it with your dress sense, sometimes,

Mum! You've got to admit that.' She knitted her eyebrows together.

'Aww darling, stop frowning, you'll scare those beautiful freckles away!' she laughed. 'You look so like your dad when he is frustrated with me – those freckles on him make him appear rugged, but on you and your pale skin, they become you.'

Rebecca scrunched her face, 'You always say that. Anyway, today, as you can imagine, Mum, my heart is heavy. Poor Lara, paying my condolences to her parents isn't something I thought I'd ever have to do!'

'It's been such a hard month for you darling. Lara and Gran is one thing and can't be helped, but Macy! I'm so shocked. That could have been me or you!'

Erin, for once, was genuinely upset. Rebecca had grown up with a sense that her mother assumed she was better than everyone else. Erin wanted the best-looking family and house, she was always immaculately dressed and expected that of her husband and daughter too. She liked to be the trendsetter and didn't take too kindly to personal criticism, even when it was her own family that said it. At times, her fiery red hair matched her personality.

Rebecca now looked at her mum in a new light, having not seen this side of her in a long time. It felt good knowing her mum had feelings like everyone else. Why did she hide behind an aura of being perfect?

Erin tidied up the cups in the sink then made a slice of toast for herself. 'Ok darling, let's leave soon. It would take at least thirty minutes to get there off-peak, but in the morning… who knows?' She shrugged her shoulders.

The journey to Lara's parents', the Henderson's house, was uneventful and Rebecca thought about her time with Lara. How they'd met in secondary school and their subsequent friendship. Then she wondered what had led her to do such a thing to herself. Suicide! That was unusual, could things have taken a turn for the worse? She'd only met her a month ago, and Lara had been jovial and was full of smiles.

Then a random thought entered her head – what if Lara had just been pretending to be happy but was miserable inside? The thought stayed in her mind for all of thirty-seconds – Lara couldn't have faked being happy about a new job with more money and a contented relationship with her boyfriend. 'We'd looked at engagement rings, for God's sake,' she whispered. There was no explanation, she would have to find out if Lara's parents knew something more. But she didn't know how she was going broach that subject with them.

When they arrived at the Henderson's house, her legs felt heavy. She dragged herself to the front door. Erin got there first and waited and watched Rebecca – she could tell her daughter was struggling to cope with it all. Mrs Henderson didn't say a word, but when Rebecca said she had loved Lara and would miss her terribly she broke down. Mr Henderson consoled her and said he couldn't understand why Lara would do such a thing. She had been in her prime of life, every-thing was going right for her and as Rebecca suspected, there appeared to be no reason for her suicide. It had even baffled her parents.

The drive home went quicker than expected. Rebecca guessed it was because she was in a daze the whole way. Listening to the Henderson's had been difficult and sad. She wondered about Matt's ordeal compared to Lara's parents; one a senseless murder, one a tragic suicide.

'Cheer up love, time will fly, and before you realise it, a year or two will have gone by,' Erin said, trying to lighten her spirits.

She nodded her head in agreement and continued looking out the window of the car.

When they got home, she texted Matt to say she was coming over, but he said there was no need because he wanted to take a nap. Rebecca wanted him to see her and let him know she was there for him. But as the date of Macy's funeral loomed closer, the more distant he was becoming. She didn't know what to do. Few people had faced such a situation – it wasn't something she could Google.

Like her father said to her, 'Just be there for him until he's ready to reach out for human company.' So, she waited for Matt, secretly dreading Macy's burial ceremony in two days' time.

After an hour of being home and being turned down by Matt, she had a bright idea to meet up with her friends Puja and Samuel. They had all met in university and Puja and Samuel had quickly become a couple. Rebecca still saw them quite often.

Puja was bubbly, and Samuel was her sponge, he soaked up all the extra enthusiasm that she brandished everywhere she went. Everyone thought they were a great match. After a few text messages between them, they agreed to come over the following day. They'd pick up Rebecca and drive over to see Matt to cheer him up. Rebecca would give Matt no excuse to refuse and she hoped they could distract him from his woes for an hour or two.

The next day, she told Matt she would be there by midday with lunch for them, she didn't tell him Puja and Samuel would also be there. Matt sounded matter-of-fact, but Rebecca didn't expect much else. When Matt realised Rebecca wasn't alone, his expression clouded over, and he glared at her. He wasn't a rude person, so he just went very quiet. Puja, Samuel and Rebecca talked about their university days. After an hour, the couple left them, promising to pay their respects at the funeral.

When they had gone, Matt scowled and said, 'You could have warned me they were coming. I told you, I didn't want any visitors!' His brown eyes bored into her. He had brown hair and thick bushy eyebrows that looked like two fat caterpillars, it gave him an endearing look. He had a large chin and forehead which he was creasing in annoyance.

'Don't be like that Matt, they came to take your

mind off tomorrow.' She was breaking into a mild sweat-she knew she had made things worse.

'It's done! So, are you going now? I'll see you at the funeral,' he said, trying to dismiss her.

She walked over to him, 'No, I'm not. I want to stay over tonight. You can't be alone,' she pleaded

'I won't be. My aunty and uncle are coming over for the night. If you had asked, I would have told you, but you assumed you would stay over. To be honest with you, I would prefer if you left. The last thing I want to see is you looking at me like a wounded animal. Lately, that's the only look I get from you. So, I hope you don't think me rude by asking you to leave.'

'He's so cold towards me,' she thought. Although his last comment had hurt her, she had to respect his wishes. She felt a distance between them she had never experienced before. What had happened to the Matt that was kind and considerate? She missed that Matt. Rebecca couldn't imagine what he was going through, with his mother being so senselessly killed, but why couldn't he see she was trying to help? Why was he so stubborn?

She called an Uber, made sure she washed the dishes and tidied up the place before she left. She went to kiss him on the lips before going, but when he turned his head and offered his cheek, she felt as though he had slapped her. She gave him a peck and left.

What Matt didn't see were the tears spilling from her eyes as she got into the Uber. She wiped them away, but as soon as she was safely in the car, they rained down her cheeks. He didn't want her anymore, she couldn't understand how their relationship, something she assumed was strong could change like that. She now suspected he would break up with her soon. It was as if he was waiting for the funeral to be over before he told her. Another thing to get upset about, the end of her two-and-a-half-year relationship with Matt!

2

A week after Macy's funeral, Matt texted Rebecca saying he wanted to talk to her about something serious and invited her over for dinner.

Rebecca was ready to head to work, but his message stopped her in her tracks and she sat down on her bed. 'It's time,' she thought. Tonight is the night he'll get rid of her! But to do it over dinner? Why not over a cup of tea or something less drawn out? She couldn't understand it, apart from telling her things weren't working out, what more was there to say? Why did he have to wring it out? Watch her break down in front of him? No, that was unlike him, but since his mother's death wasn't his normal self at all.

Over the last week, after the funeral, she had confided in Puja. Puja had tried to reassure her it was only the death of his mother that was making things difficult for their relationship. She told Rebecca to bide her time and stick with him. She reminded her what a fun-loving guy he used to be and that he needed time, so he could process these dark days. Puja knew how much Matt loved her and how devoted he was to her, so she assured Rebecca that he will gradually return to his old self.

But after getting the text message today, Rebecca questioned whether she could still cling to him. She didn't lack self-esteem, she knew she could get over it in time, but she didn't want to lose him either, after nearly three years of going out together. She'd invested so much of her time with him and she loved him. He needed her – she had to make him see that.

Rebecca went to work that day troubled by Matt's text. She tried to dismiss it and concentrate on work, but it wasn't easy.

'Morning, beautiful,' Frank called out to her when he came out of his office. He'd been in telephone meetings since she'd got in. She looked up, forcing a smile. He was a handsome man in his early thirties, with a slightly tanned skin that gave him a Mediterranean appearance. He was wearing black tailored trousers, a fitted white shirt and a navy tie. Frank knew how to dress and he always took pride in his appearance.

'Hey you, all ok?' There was a touch of impatience in her voice, she tried not to look at his face, her eyes scanned his body, which, she could see was lean and toned, he was obviously a regular at the gym.

Frank was the nephew of the owner, Logan Pearson.

Apart from being the office manager, he was also someone she had been out with briefly. When Rebecca had got together with Matt, she knew Frank still had a soft spot for her. He had taken her dismissal hard, so he transferred to the Scotland office for six months to separate himself from working with her. It had been a good decision. On his return, he'd stayed away from Rebecca to give Matt and her the space they needed.

'Yes, everything is brilliant.'

He stared at her with his striking hazel eyes. 'But you don't look ok, is anything wrong?' he asked, running his hands through his short, jet-black hair.

'Nope, did I say anything was wrong?' She forced a smile.

'But you look troubled,' he said with genuine concern.

'Well, I'm fine, Frank,' she snapped, trying to get rid of him.

'Rebecca…' He elongated her name to emphasise it. 'Something's wrong isn't it? Don't hide it from me.' He said, giving her a half-smile. He knew things had been difficult at home lately, with her recent losses. He had struggled to stop loving her but he couldn't – the best thing he could do as her manager and friend, was to be as professional as possible.

'I'm fine Frank, thanks for asking,' she said and shifted back to her computer screen.

He peered at her for a few extra seconds, studying her. She was pretty without trying, with no make-up, she looked fresh, clean and virtuous. Today, she was wearing a tight-fitting cream dress with a pink and red floral printed border on the hem and neckline, and a matching floral belt she'd tied in a bow at the back. She'd gathered her long red hair at the nape of her neck in a ponytail to keep it out the way. She always came to the office with her hair tied. He looked at the fair skin on her neck and shoulders and smiled, even they were peppered with freckles.

He didn't get a further response from her, so he gave up and left her to it. But he knew something distracted her and it wasn't just her grief. She would explain everything when she was ready. She often did that when things were tough and she wanted advice from him rather than her normal circle of friends.

Frank had met Rebecca when she'd started working for his uncle's Scottish Highlands cottage rental business. When he'd joined, they'd teamed up so she could teach him how to manage properties in her portfolio. It wasn't difficult, but they had to follow set timescales once properties got rented and then he had to learn what to do once they were available again. The next step in the process was how to prepare it for another letting. It was time-consuming work that required attention to detail and they had to follow company procedures. Rebecca taught him at a slow pace to make sure he understood everything. He'd spent a lot of time with her, she was funny and didn't give him special treatment just because he was the boss's nephew. He liked that.

After a few months, he'd plucked up the courage to

ask her on a date, and they went on a few more outings. Rebecca told him she was reluctant to take the friendship further because she didn't want her colleagues thinking she was given special treatment by the owner's nephew. Frank had taken things slow with her, so he didn't frighten her off – they even kissed a few times, but nothing more. Rebecca said she loved her job and wasn't willing to take that risk, in case it jeopardised things at work.

After Rebecca started dating Matt, Frank's uncle, Logan, swapped places with him so Frank could get a clean break from her. Frank moved to the Scottish office to clear his mind. But it wasn't enough time to get over her.

Frank was eight years older than Rebecca and she liked the fact that he was more mature than her friends. Today, he got back into his office and pretended to work, glancing over at her now and again. She had changed a lot this past month, she looked thinner than normal and sometimes distracted from her duties.

He got busy with work meetings and forgot about her. By the time he remembered and went out to check on her, she had left. She claimed she was feeling unwell – he didn't believe that. He suspected something was going on with her, he would find out soon enough.

'**D**amn him!' she swore. Why was Frank so inquisitive? How could he sense she was troubled by just looking at her? It was annoying, and she was fed up with his magnifying glass on her every time she got upset. Right now, though, Frank was the least of her issues. She was more worried about what Matt wanted to discuss with her. She went home, had a long relaxing bath, changed into jeans and a pink cotton top she felt at ease in. She didn't want Matt thinking she'd tried too hard, although she was feeling down about their possible breakup. She still loved Matt, even if he didn't love her anymore. But she would not beg him either – she was a confident woman who didn't depend on the reassurances of being with a man.

She got to his house at the agreed time and he opened his arms to grab a hug when he saw her. That was the last thing she expected, but her surprise didn't end there. Matt's aunty Cathleen and uncle Robert were there too. She didn't understand, she'd expected them to be alone. Maybe Matt wanted back-up of his family. It made little sense to her.

'Hello, Aunty Cath and Uncle Rob, what a surprise to see you both here. I expected you to have gone back to Manchester after the funeral.' She realised she was babbling, but she didn't care.

'Hi darling,' Cathleen said. 'No, we had to make sure our sweet Matt was settled in before we went back. We couldn't leave him in the lurch.' Cathleen looked like she'd slapped on more make-up than usual.

'No, of course not,' Rebecca said, trying not to stare at the dusky pink eyeshadow Cathleen had plastered on.

'Let's crack open the champagne,' said Robert, to break up the awkward silence.

'Champagne?' she asked Matt.

'Oh yeah, I told you I had something to tell to you, didn't I?' he said with a sly grin.

Rebecca looked strangely at him.

Matt called out, 'Uncle Rob, hang on a minute.'

Robert stopped and turned around with a big smile on his face.

Cathleen then said, 'Go on Matt.'

Their sudden burst of unusual behaviour confused Rebecca. She watched them, not knowing what to say. Then Matt spoke.

'Rebecca, you have been so patient with me over these past few months. It has been difficult for us, but I hope you know that I appreciate it.'

'Hmmm... that's ok, Matt. What happened was awful and I wanted to be there for you.' Why was he calling her Rebecca? He called her Bec. This wasn't the way she'd expected he would break up with her. With an audience!

'Yeah, it's been terrible,' he said, looking down at his shoes all off a sudden, studying them as if there was something interesting to look at.

Nobody spoke. He then took her hands in his and said, 'This isn't how I wanted to do this, but I didn't want to wait any longer.'

Rebecca looked at him wide-eyed, her heart started to beat faster as he got down on one knee.

'Rebecca, will you marry me?' He asked staring up at her, now beginning to blush.

Cathleen and Rebecca both shrieked at the same moment for different reasons: Cathleen in excitement and Rebecca in shock.

She pulled her hand out of his. 'What are you doing, Matt?' she whispered, once she gained her composure and not wanting his aunt and uncle to hear.

'Proposing, what else?' He beamed at her, willing her to say 'Yes'.

'But I thought…' she trailed off.

'Thought what?' he asked.

'Oh nothing,' she said, giving him a huge smile.

'Well, give him an answer girl!' Cathleen begged.

They waited for her to accept. But she was awestruck – the opposite of what she expected to happen had happened!

'Well?' he asked, still bent on one knee.

'Yes!' she squealed, he rose and hugged her tightly. He kissed her then picked her up, twirling her around, making her scream in delight.

'Put me down, Matt, for God's sake. You'll do your back in!'

Cathleen and Robert congratulated them, Robert got the champagne, and she realised why they were still here. They'd wanted to make sure Matt had someone permanent in his life once they left.

Rebecca joined in on the merry-making, but she was still in a daze at the turn of events. Never in a million years had she expected Matt to propose, but hell, she was glad she had said yes. She hadn't seen him this happy in a long time – she'd almost forgotten what he looked like when he smiled. In the past, they had talked about marriage and children, they were excited to one day make a life together. But she'd never expected the day would come so soon, with the way Matt had been behaving lately.

She was over the moon that they were still a couple and she drove home happy as a lark. He tried to persuade her to stay the night, but she didn't have her work clothes with her, so she refused.

'Tell them you're sick, and take the day off tomorrow,' he encouraged her, but she still didn't want to.

'I like working there, I wouldn't want to stress them because there was one less body on the ground.'

'Well, one day won't do them any harm, Bec, will it?'

'Go on, darling,' Cathleen coxed her.

'As much as I want to, I can't. I will stay over at the weekend as usual.' She tried to sound chirpy.

He sighed and gave up. 'Ok, fine, but take a day off next week. Let's drive out to Kent.

'What a great idea,' said Robert.

To get them all off her back, she agreed. She didn't like to take random days off, she liked working and she didn't agree with leaving her colleagues in the lurch. She felt a sense of responsibility and didn't want to let

Frank down – she didn't want him thinking she was irresponsible.

Her parents were still awake watching TV, when she got home. She walked over to them, her eyes shining.

'Mum, Dad, guess what?' Without waiting for an answer, she blurted out, 'I'm engaged to Matt! He asked me tonight!' She was smiling from ear to ear.

Finn jumped up from his chair to hug her. After giving her a burly squeeze, he let her go. They were both laughing.

Erin smiled at them and got up to embrace Rebecca. But her demeanour did not go unnoticed

'What's wrong darling?' Finn asked Erin, looking at her with narrowed eyes.

'It's nothing,' she murmured under her breath.

'Yes, it is, come on, Mum? Why aren't you happy for me?' she asked, frowning.

'I am, my darling, it's just…' She trailed off.

'Just what?' questioned Finn.

'… Well, don't you think it's odd he proposed so soon after his mother's death and only a week after her burial?'

'Darling…' Finn started but didn't get to finish.

Rebecca burst out, 'There it is, I knew it. You never want the best for me, do you, Mum? You crave to be the centre of attention all the time, can't you stop being so self-obsessed for once and be happy for me?'

Erin attempted to hug her, 'Please darling, I love you. I want you to be happy, I do.'

Rebecca stepped back, not wanting Erin to hold her,

'Well I don't think you do! Anyway, thanks for your support. Dad, I'm going to bed, happy knowing I will soon marry someone I love.' Saying that, she stormed off.

Tears pricked at the back of her eyes as she got to her bedroom. That was typical behaviour from her mother, as usual – unfeeling and cold.

3

W hen Rebecca was out of earshot, Finn turned to his wife, 'What's wrong with you, Erin? She's the only daughter we have left, for God's sake!' He was pacing the living room floor and ranting at the same time. 'As usual, you are hell bent on destroying everyone in this family! First, you alienate your Scottish relatives from us, now you are doing the same to Rebecca.'

Erin stared at Finn and kept her voice low as she snarled at him, 'I told you never to speak about our life in Scotland! You promised, so shut the hell up before she hears you! Anyway, I can't help it. I do find it bizarre that he should ask at a time like this. Don't you think it's strange?'

'Frankly, I don't. Time like what?' He yelled, he wanted to talk about their estranged Scottish family, but she distracted him from doing so by the engagement talk.

'Macy passed away under tragic circumstances, he has only recently buried her. It's too soon, Finn,' she pleaded.

'Well, they don't think so, do they? Have you considered he could be lonely and now realises life is too short? Maybe he doesn't want to waste any more time waiting. Sometimes fate throws things at you and it changes your whole existence. He has always loved her. If he didn't ask her now, he would have done so later, anyway.'

She didn't speak, it was as if she'd withdrawn from their conversation. He waited there, looking at her. He hoped his explanations had made her understand.

After half a minute, she said, 'I guess. Well, what's done is done. I'm tired, and I'm going to bed. Goodnight, love.'

Finn stood there, watching her spurn him as she strode upstairs. The cheek of that woman! When arguments didn't go her way, she walked off. Their marriage wasn't perfect, but Erin pretended it was to everyone outside of their house. After Rebecca was born, they'd been happy for a while, but then, like a flip of the coin, his whole life had changed and they'd moved from Scotland to London. Luckily, Rebecca had been too young to understand much, but the problems they'd faced then had brought them close to breaking up.

Things weren't right ever again. They'd got better, but it had cost them a lot of pain. Finn always thought he had it worse, Erin seemed to be unfazed by it. But it was in the past, and there was no point dwelling on it now.

He did, however, see a much colder, more calculated Erin. He learned, over time, that every move she made had been planned and controlled. Like she was the chess master and everyone else were pawns on her board, to do with what she wished. Despite that, Finn never hated her, but he wasn't in love with her either, they had enough mutual respect for their marriage to work. He decided, long ago, that he had to try, for Rebecca's sake. He'd lost a lot by moving to London, and he could lose a lot more if he left Erin, so he shut up and put up with her demands.

Erin tried to make amends in the morning by sounding bubbly and offering to make Rebecca pancakes, but she refused, saying she would grab breakfast en route to work. Her dad had left extra early to go to work too. He texted Rebecca to explain he'd had words with her mother and he would see her later.

Rebecca had a loving relationship with her father, but there were times he ignored the topic at hand. She worried that her mother had poisoned her father against her engagement to Matt last night. That is what Erin did, make her dad stay quiet! There were several times her father looked as if he had something to tell her, but he always changed the subject. Especially if her mother was around. What did he want to say to her that he couldn't in front of his wife?

Rebecca got to work with a smile on her face and Matt's mother's engagement ring on her finger. She told nobody, she wanted to see if they noticed it. Frank had to attend meetings all day, so he wasn't in the office – he would have guessed straight away!

Once settled in her workspace and logged on to her computer, she texted Puja.

'Guess what? I got big news. Can we meet for lunch?'

Puja worked nearby, and they sometimes lunched together. Rebecca enjoyed those lunches with her. Within minutes, she replied:

'Of course, you know how I enjoy a good gossip!!! Lol. What time?'

'Just after one at our usual cafe?'

'Great, see you then. Can't wait!'

Rebecca put a smiley and a monkey covering its mouth emoji. Then she giggled. Puja would be as shocked as she was when she found out.

By lunchtime, all her colleagues had heard the news of her engagement. Frank found out, even though he was out of the office and tried to ring her – she recognised his number, but she didn't pick up. 'Oh no,' she thought, he would try to sound happy for her, but she suspected it would hurt him and she didn't want to deal with his complicated feelings right now.

When she met Puja, she tried keeping her surprise

hidden for as long as possible, even though she was dying to say something. Rebecca ordered the salmon croissant with hot chocolate, but Puja just wanted cheese on toast.

'That's not a proper lunch, Puja,' she protested, expecting Puja to order more. Today, she wanted to pay for lunch.

'I'm careful when I eat out Bec, you should know that by now. I forgot my EpiPen and knowing my luck, with my stupid allergy, I could get a reaction just looking at a nut!'

Rebecca nodded her head in understanding then laughed and said, 'Well you are a nut, anyway!'

Puja slapped her hand in jest and they laughed together, 'You're so naughty, Bec!'

When Rebecca finally told her about the engagement, Puja screamed in surprise. She hugged her tight and said, 'And there you were, panicking he would dump you! Let me see the ring!'

Rebecca offered her left hand, 'God, look at this rock, it's exquisite!'

On her hand sat a white gold engagement ring which had a 1.2 carat, brilliant cut solitaire diamond ring with three smaller diamonds on each of the shoulders, giving it even more sparkle.

'It's beautiful, isn't it? It was his mother's ring.'

'I am sure his mother is beaming with happiness up there, looking down at her son and the lovely lady that agreed to become his wife. She liked you, Bec.'

'And I liked her, poor thing.'

They both sat there, reflecting for a few moments. Then Puja said, 'Heck, we should celebrate. Let's have a small get-together for your engagement?'

'Yeah, great idea, but let me run it by Matt first. He may not be ready for a party yet.'

'What? You're engaged for five minutes and you're already under the thumb?'

'Don't be silly, Puja. He just lost his mother. I'm not sure he's ready yet.'

Puja nodded her head and smiled. 'I'm just teasing you, Bec. I understand, and yes, definitely ask him if he is ready. God, if I lost my mum like that or even through sickness or something, I wouldn't cope with it. It's great that his aunt and uncle were there, too, babe.'

'Yeah, it was. Well, we'd better get back to work – it's late. I'll text you later or in a few days to tell you what Matt says about the party idea.'

Rebecca paid for their lunch and they headed back talking until they parted ways. Rebecca's spirits rose again. After her mother's damp reception of her engagement last night, she'd started to question Matt's motives too. She wondered if he was just going insane, or did he seriously want to get married? She shelved these thoughts after meeting Puja because she didn't think that their engagement was strange.

F rank had been between meetings when he'd called Lisa back. She was the accountant at their office and he'd had several missed calls from her already. He'd guessed something was amiss, so had rung her. She told him Rebecca's news, which was the last thing he'd been expecting to hear. He took the news of the engagement well and told Lisa he would call Rebecca to congratulate her and thanked her for telling him.

When his call ended, he flopped onto the one chair in the room, deflated. He was losing his Frey and there was nothing he could do about it. He should have heeded his uncle's suggestions and stayed in the Scotland office instead of coming back. His uncle must have known he still had hidden feelings for Rebecca. Pretending he was over her, he'd even fooled himself into believing it!

His next meeting was in five minutes, so he rushed out to join it. It was not a productive meeting because he kept losing the thread of the conversations and stared into space a lot. He fiddled with his pen and doodled on his pad, all the while daydreaming about Rebecca.

'Frank, are you ok?' asked a delegate.

'Hmm, sorry Ross. I'm coming down with some- thing. I don't think I am taking any of this in,' he said, rubbing his forehead.

'You looked troubled, Frank. Why don't you leave and get some rest? I can give you a rundown when you feel better.' Ross sounded concerned. This was unlike Frank.

He excused himself, got in his car and sat there, contemplating everything. Something crossed his mind that got him excited, so he fished out his phone and Googled a few things. He loaded his satellite navigation to his required destination and set off in haste.

When he reached his destination, he didn't hesitate. He got out of his car, scanned the neighbourhood to see if anyone was around and then walked to the house tapping on the door three times. There was no answer, so he stepped back to appraise the house. It seemed quiet, like nobody was home. He knocked again and waited. Still no answer. He then thought maybe this wasn't a good idea and made his way back to his car.

After taking five strides towards his car, someone from behind him asked, 'What do you want?'

He turned around and saw Matt, looking worse for wear. His hair looked dishevelled and his clothes hastily put on.

He said, 'Hi, Matt it's me, Frank.'

'Oh, I know who you are, Rebecca's boss.'

'Yes, that's me.'

'What do you want? Rebecca's not here.' Matt sounded harsh, snapping at Frank.

Frank walked back towards the house, 'I heard about your engagement to Rebecca.'

'Oh, that.' Matt smiled. 'Yeah, it's great.'

'Look, I'm sorry for your loss, Matt, but are you sure this is what you want?' he blurted.

Matt's smile disappeared. 'Pardon me, but the last

person I will take advice from is Bec's boss, who I am certain still loves her!'

Frank frowned, 'Think about it, Matt, is it just a knee-jerk reaction after losing your mother? If that hadn't happened, I can guarantee you wouldn't have asked her to marry you.'

Matt walked the last few steps between them. 'You've got a fucking nerve, coming here to lecture me like that! Do you think I want advice from you? Who do you think you are?' He was starting to shout.

Frank was getting angry too. 'Someone that cares about Rebecca, you shouldn't drag her into your sorry world just because you're lonely. Man, look at you! You haven't been out the house in days. No pride in your appearance at all. I hope she sees sense before it's too late!' he yelled back.

'Fuck you and your thoughts. I feel sorry for you, coming here like a beggar, I know you want her for yourself. Use your brain, Frank. You're the one with nothing and I've got her. There is fuck all you can do about it mate, so get out of my face and never come to my house again.'

'The only beggar is you, and I am not your "*mate*". I'm just here to tell you to leave her out of your sorry life. She deserves better.'

Matt came up to Frank's face and shouted, 'Better? You think you are better than me? Just because your uncle owns that fucking company Rebecca works in? Newsflash, Frank – your uncle is the owner and you are a normal worker there, nothing special!'

Frank stepped back, 'I am better, I have a good job, I take care of myself and I care for her. All I came here to do is get some assurance from you that you will take care of her too.'

Matt raised his arm to Frank's chest and pushed him back. 'Fuck you, and fuck off from here before I call the police, pretty boy!'

Frank glared at him, why couldn't Matt see that he was only looking out for Rebecca? He suddenly felt like punching him right on the nose. He knew he was fit enough to take him on. But he also knew Rebecca would never forgive him if he did that, so he stepped back, still scowling at Matt.

'Yeah, go on, run, and don't think I won't tell Rebecca about your little visit. Guess who won't be getting an invitation to the wedding, loser!' he taunted.

Frank spun around and got into his car. He could hear Matt shouting behind him.

'Go on, fuck off, you're nothing but a coward, running away like that. You will never get her! Ever!'

Frank stepped on the accelerator and sped off. His blood was boiling.

4

———

'*It's all a mess!*' Frank shouted to himself when he got home. There was no point going back to the office. He was in a bad way. Rebecca would hate him when she found out what had happened. All he had wanted to do was talk to Matt, reason with him, and check that his motives for marrying Rebecca were genuine. He'd even expected Matt to invite him in for a coffee to discuss it! 'What a fool,' he muttered. He should have known Matt would be annoyed.

But one thing was clear, Matt wasn't of sound mind. Frank had to speak to someone, so he rang his uncle, Logan. He was close to his uncle, they had similar personalities, he was understanding and could advise him too.

'What the hell were you doing there, Frank?' Logan hollered from the other end of the phone. 'You are better than that! Why you felt the need to talk to him is beyond me! The man recently lost his mother and under difficult circumstances. Now you've made things worse for him.'

Logan's response stunned Frank, he'd expected support, not a tongue lashing. But his uncle made sense. If anyone had reacted in a knee-jerk way, it was him.

When his uncle simmered down, he said he wanted to travel to London. Frank protested and said he was handling it, but Logan was insistent. 'Frank, besides some work I need to take care of in London, I also need to be sure you are ok. You're like a son to me, I will never have any children of my own, you mean the world to me.'

He was glad his uncle couldn't see him. Tears were falling from his eyes. He tried to stay strong, but in the comfort of his home, he let down his guard. Logan could tell he'd touched a nerve and told Frank to hang tight. Despite his tears, Frank felt more positive after talking to Logan. Things were going to be much better with his uncle around.

'W*hat the hell?*' Rebecca yelled at Matt. 'The man still has a weak spot for me. You should have tried to be more tactful towards him!'

Rebecca couldn't understand what had happened between the men that afternoon. Frank shouldn't have interfered and Matt could have told him to mind his own business and be done with it. Now, the whole neigh-bourhood and God knows who else will have heard how two men had argued about her. 'God, it's like a TV drama!' She mumbled to herself.

'I tried,' Matt yelled back, 'but he had no right to come here, with his condescending attitude. Prancing like he fucking owns the place, not to mention you!'

'Ok fine, Matt, I love you, and I do agree with you, but did you have to be so rude?'

'I wasn't rude, I told him he was a loser and he wouldn't be invited to our wedding!' he said, laughing.

'That's awful, Matt, how could you?' She was mortified.

He continued laughing, 'Yeah, that was satisfying, I can tell you that much.'

Rebecca was afraid to ask, but she did anyway, 'And what did he say to that?'

'Nothing, he looked like he wanted to punch me, man, he was mad!' he chuckled.

'Well, that's not nice. Now I have to face him, he's still my manager!' Her heart went out to Frank. His actions had been so out of character. He was normally self-assured, independent and strong. She hadn't realised he still held such deep feelings for her. She needed to speak to him and make it clear he was never to approach Matt again. She would also apologise for Matt's cruel remarks. But she wouldn't tell Matt – she wanted to make peace from all sides.

Matt looked sly, 'So will you search for a new job? I'll support you if you choose to stop working completely, of course.'

'No – why would I need another job? Do you

expect Frank to sack me after this?' She anxiously chewed her lower lip.

'Of course not, he won't sack you, he wouldn't dare after what he did. No, I mean you might prefer to work somewhere else because of him. He still loves you – why else would he behave the way he did?'

'I don't want to work elsewhere! If he has feelings for me, then he hasn't shown them till now. What happened shouldn't affect my work at all.' She was surprised that he'd even suggest it.

Matt was getting annoyed, 'How can you go back there, knowing he has a problem with us? Think, Rebecca!' His voice was abrasive.

'He had a problem with you, not me. You can't expect me to give up a job I love because the two of you had a minor tiff.'

'Minor tiff?' he barked.

'Stop shouting, I can hear you! Yes, what happened between you had nothing to do with me!' She could feel her face growing red.

'Are you crazy – it had everything to do with you.'

'Well, I didn't encourage him, until this incident, I never knew he had such intense feelings for me.' She whispered the last few words.

'It is what it is.' His voice softened too and then he asked tentatively, 'So, are you going to hand in your resignation?'

'I like my job, so no, I'm not.' She was hoping he wouldn't make her feel guilty for her decision.

'Is there another reason you choose to stay?' He was

pushing his luck, but he was desperate for her to leave her job. He hated the thought of Frank being anywhere near her.

'Like what?' She wasn't sure what he was getting at.

'You can tell me, I will understand, I promise.'

'I can't tell you because I don't know what you're talking about,' she snapped.

'If you still fancy him, say so. The man was once a teen model – he's handsome. So, I can see the attraction that you or other people might have for him!' His voice, once again cold.

'Are you drunk?' she laughed. 'If not, then you are kidding right?' She was smiling, but the stare he gave her was chilling, she could see he wasn't joking – was he really trying to find out if she wanted to be with Frank instead of him?

He stood there glaring at her.

'Matt, let's leave this subject and for clarification, I will say: I love you, not him. I love my job because of what I do, not because I prefer to be with Frank, and no, I won't ever let a man guilt me into changing a decision because he is insecure!' It sounded harsh, but she had to set the ground rules.

'Is it because you like him chasing you?' his tone was sharp again.

'How dare you!' she gasped. Tears sprang to her eyes and within seconds spilled onto her cheeks. He continued to stare at her, a cold unfeeling gaze. This was a new Matt – the passing of his mother had changed him

– and Rebecca wondered if she was going to be able to deal with him.

'I'm going home,' she whispered, looking down at her feet so he couldn't see how much he'd hurt her.

He turned away and made no effort to stop her.

Rebecca spent her evening pondering the whole conversation she'd had with Matt. She wondered now, if her mother's doubts might be justified. Could this Matt differ from the person she had loved before? Had Macy's death affected him so much that it would change him forever?

She froze as she considered the dreaded question, the one her mother had raised – was this engagement too soon after Macy's death? What if it was? She required to speak to Puja, she asked her to bring Samuel along too. He'd be able to give a male perspective.

It was a restless night for Rebecca, she tried to relax, but the next morning she got up still tired. It was Saturday, she'd arranged to meet up with Puja and Samuel for lunch. She glanced at her phone – as yet, there were still no messages from Matt. 'Sod him,' she muttered under her breath.

As soon as Puja saw Rebecca, she hugged her fiercely. Samuel stared at her as if she was a stray dog.

Puja spoke first. 'Our baby, Bec, look at you! First fight as an engaged couple?' she said, feeling sorry for her.

Rebecca told her they'd argued and enlightened her on the details. When she'd finished her story, neither of them spoke as they let the details of what she'd said, sink in.

Samuel broke the silence. 'Frank was wrong to reason with Matt, but maybe he had a point, now you mention Matt's behaviour. Obviously, Matt's my friend, so I'd prefer to defend him. But I, too, have noticed a change in him. It may be because of what happened to his mother, so I am not blaming him, but I would question if this is the Matt you wish to marry.'

Both the girls looked at each other in surprise. Samuel was usually on the quiet side, but he was also very intelligent. So, when he expressed an opinion, it carried weight.

Puja said, 'I agree with Sam and to some extent, your mum has been right all along.'

Rebecca looked at both but said nothing. They were considerate enough to let her reflect on their opinions. Finally, she spoke, 'I guess the best thing to do is wait and see. I don't want to make hasty decisions and ruin a relationship without exploring my options. I need to watch Matt over the next few weeks and see if he changes back. One thing's for sure, he's not the man I loved a few months ago.'

'You have to take one day at a time, that boy might take ages to return,' said Puja.

'And what should I say to Frank? I haven't seen him since their argument. I want to tell him to stay away from Matt.

Samuel answered, 'He will be going through a hard time at the moment too, but I agree you still need to make it clear to him that what he did was out of line. What about taking one or two weeks' leave so that the dust can settle? That way, Matt won't feel like he lost, and neither will you, with the bonus you won't need to see Frank for a while.'

'And that's why I love you, my bright spark. Brains and beauty!' Puja burst out with glee.

'I have to say,' Rebecca said, smiling at them, 'that's a great plan. I'll ask for time off when I go back next week.'

She looked at her phone – no messages from Matt. She decided she'd have to be the one to make the first move. If it wasn't for his bereavement, she might have given up a lot quicker. She thought she should wait until she got home before deciding.

After talking about her dilemma, the three of them had gone on to chat about other things and Rebecca had found relief in the light conversation. They parted company soon afterwards. After leaving them, Rebecca didn't feel like going straight home, so she took a train to her favourite bookshop in central London.

When she got back home, her mother yelled, 'Hi love, I'm in the kitchen making tea. You want me to make you a cup?'

Rebecca debated whether to tell her mother about her issues with Matt or not. She didn't want her to say, 'I told you so!'

'Yes, please,' she shouted back. She put the books

45

she'd bought on the coffee table and walked into the kitchen.

'So, how was your lunch with Puja and Samuel?' Erin asked as soon as she saw her.

'Yeah good, they're fun to be with and then I lost myself in a bookshop in central.'

'Buy anything?'

'Yes, three books.'

'Oh, nice.' Erin remarked. Then silence.

Erin wasn't a book reader, she preferred watching the story on the screen. Rebecca's father, Finn, however, loved books, and if she'd told him she'd visited the bookshop, he would have asked what the book was about. However, if Rebecca told her mother she'd bought make-up or nail polish, her mum's eyes would light up, and she'd insist on seeing everything.

When they were both sat down, Erin asked, 'So how is Matt? You're pretty quiet about him.'

Rebecca hesitated for a few moments but saw no point in hiding the 'Frank and Matt Show' and told her the whole story. She omitted the argument she had with Matt later.

Erin was surprised too, 'Well, well, well, Frank stood up for what he wants!'

'He doesn't want me Mum and he didn't say that. He voiced the same concerns you had when I told you Matt and I had got engaged. It wasn't any more than that!' she snarled.

'If he didn't care, why did he behave like that? That boy loves you, Rebecca. He is so handsome and smart. I prefer Frank to your snivelling Matt,' she said, wrinkling her nose with disgust.

'You, Mum, can prefer anyone you want, but it's my life and I choose Matt!'

Erin was scared she might alienate both Rebecca and Finn again, so she left the topic alone. 'Fine, you're right. It's your choice.'

Rebecca was glad and surprised. Most times, her mother was like a Rottweiler. She tore everyone to shreds till she got her way. Maybe she is getting weaker as she gets older. Rebecca smiled at the thought. She could never say that – Erin couldn't bear to be reminded she was ageing.

After tea with her mother, she headed up to change into comfortable clothes. While she was in her room, she texted Matt.

'Hi Matt, how are you? I hate it when we fight. Can we talk? I am worried about you.'

She hesitated before she pressed the 'send' button. Her instincts were telling her not to send it because she'd done nothing wrong. But her heart ached for Matt, alone, with no one. After a brief inner battle, she pressed it. Let's see what he comes back with.

Nothing! Matt hadn't replied and that angered her. It had been an hour since she'd sent her message to him. In that time, she'd had a long bath and pottered around her room, putting clothes she hadn't worn back into the wardrobe.

She'd not bothered with her phone whilst it was charging on her bedside table, she hoped that he was sending a flurry of messages saying he was sorry too, and he missed her. So, she wasn't happy when she saw the blank screen – no notifications.

Rebecca remembered the books she'd bought earlier and picked one to read, but she couldn't get into it. She couldn't keep her mind off Matt and started wondering whether agreeing to marry him had been such a good decision.

Her thoughts shifted to Frank. Yes, he was quite handsome, and he had a soft spot for her, but what else? Until now, she had focused her attention only on Matt, but as she dwelled on Frank, she began to see a different picture. All the signs were there; the man doted on her and she hadn't even noticed. If he wasn't around, she didn't like it. Not only did she not want him to withdraw from this office to go back to Scotland, she now suspected she didn't want to abandon her job, as Matt suggested, because of him. She didn't want to leave Frank!

The realisation hit her like a brick thrown at her head and confused her. Was Matt right? Might she still have feelings for Frank and not want to admit it to herself? He was her comfort blanket, but was there more? But she needed to concentrate on her issues with Matt before figuring out her possible feelings for Frank.

It was still early, she grabbed a quick bite of dinner downstairs and nipped back up to her bedroom, unnoticed by her parents. She needed to be alone. On returning to her room, she checked her phone – Matt still hadn't messaged her. In anger, she switched her phone off and flung it onto the chair opposite her bed and settled back to read. She decided not to bother with her phone again tonight.

The more she pondered Matt's rejection of her, the angrier she got, but she was resolved not to look at her phone, it was the only way she could relax. She carried on reading, and after a while, dozed off, her book falling to the side.

Rebecca woke up with a fright. Someone was frantically knocking on her bedroom door. She sat bolt upright in bed, 'Mum?' she screamed.

'Yes, it's me, Rebecca – open up.' Her mother shouted back.

She pushed her covers away and jumped out of bed, unlatching her door to her waiting parents. She looked from one to the other in panic, fearing the worst.

'Oh, my God, has something happened to Matt?' she asked.

A hundred thoughts passed through her head in the fraction of a second they took to answer. She hated herself for being angry at him. She should have tried harder, she could have done something… but her thoughts were interrupted.

'No, it's not Matt,' said Finn in a quiet voice.

'Who then?' she asked, dreading that he would say it was Frank.

Her mum answered her question. 'It's Puja, darling,

they have admitted her to hospital after she suffered a severe allergic reaction.'

'Oh noooo…' she said, backing away from them whilst she covered her mouth with her hands.

Finn said, 'She is unconscious but still alive, Frey. Don't cry, she's in good hands, and they're looking after her.' He walked over to hug her, but she couldn't hug him back. She stood there in his arms in shock, tears silently coursing down her cheeks.

R ebecca dressed hurriedly, in faded blue jeans and a somber grey top and got to the hospital at just after nine. Her father declared she was in no fit state to drive, so he offered to take her there. She fretted all the way to there. She kept thinking that if her phone hadn't been turned off she would have found out about Puja. There were still no messages from Matt, but that was the least of her worries.

At the intensive care unit, she saw Puja's parents, Mr and Mrs Khan, Samuel and Molly, another old university friend. Mrs Khan was sitting on a chair, looking down at her feet, holding her head in her hands. At first glance, Rebecca thought they had lost Puja. Samuel came over to her, and she looked at him, forehead wrinkled and tears streaming down her face.

'Is she?'

Samuel shook his head, 'No, she's still the same.' He was crying now.

Rebecca hugged him and rubbed his back like a child that has lost its favourite toy. 'Don't worry Samuel, she will pull through. She is like an ox, that girl!' She tried to sound jovial but was failing miserably. Then she added, 'Let me go over to her parents to say I'm here.'

Puja's parents looked as if they were in a different world, somewhere far away from reality. She could tell that now was not a good time to approach them.

'Not now, Bec, they fear for her life, like us. I can't imagine their pain. Let them be with their own thoughts for now,' Samuel said wiping the tears from his eyes.

'Ok, Samuel.'

They sat on a pair of chairs at the opposite end of the waiting area to Puja's parents. After a while, Rebecca asked, 'So what happened, Samuel?'

Samuel began by sobbing before he even spoke, 'Bec… Bec, it's all my fault.'

Rebecca was concerned. 'What do you mean, Samuel?'

His chest heaved as he tried to suppress his tears, 'I hurried… her out… the flat so we could… go to dinner,' he hiccupped through his sobs.

'So, what's that got to do with it?' she enquired.

'I was hungry, Bec, I told her to hurry the hell up, so I could eat! So, when she changed her main bag to a smaller one, she forgot her EpiPen.' He broke down.

Poor Samuel, he'd always loved Puja more than she loved him. She was bright, intelligent and funny. Added to that, she had waist-length dark brown hair, beautiful brown skin, and big dark eyes. Samuel called her 'his Arabian princess' even though she laughed and said she had an Indian heritage, but he paid no attention.

Samuel was a contrast to Puja, had light brown hair and the palest skin, which brought out his freckles. His eyes were blue and his nose larger than he would have liked. He always seemed nerdy to Rebecca because he spent a lot of time reading.

Samuel's family were not from London, so he had nobody there to support him, which is why Rebecca stood by him. She held him as he cried, telling him it wasn't his fault, but he kept insisting it was. She felt as though Samuel had held his emotions in check until now. He'd stayed strong because Puja's parents were finding it hard, but with her here, he was comfortable enough to cry. She hadn't seen him so vulnerable before. It broke her heart.

As his sobs subsided, she noticed Molly sitting at the opposite side of the room, holding Mrs Khan's hand. This confused Rebecca – Molly wasn't that close a friend to Puja, so why had Samuel called her?

When he had calmed down, she gently asked again, 'How exactly did it happen, Samuel?'

She offered him another tissue. He wiped his tears, blew his nose, then replied, 'I'm not sure, Bec. We're always so careful when we eat out, usually choosing places we have built a trust with. Last night, we went to Pizza Palace – they have a good reputation for looking after customers with nut allergies. They even have a separate menu, specially for food allergy sufferers. We've never had an issue with their food in the past.

'The restaurant was busy, so I'm not sure if they got our orders mixed up or not. It was a severe reaction, straight after she took her first bite. God Bec, I fumbled around her bag looking for the bloody EpiPen then realised it wasn't in there.

'She mentioned she was having trouble breathing, through her gasps for air she said her throat was getting increasingly tighter. She tried to scream for her auto-injector, and I couldn't think straight. The customers gathered all around, wanting to help, but there was nothing they could do. One of the staff or the guests called for an ambulance, which came within ten minutes. Luckily, whilst we were waiting, a passerby noticed the commotion in the restaurant and came in to look. When he found out she was in anaphylactic shock, he gave us his EpiPen. It may have saved her life.' He teared up again.

Rebecca wanted to cry so much but held it together for his sake. She asked, 'What have the doctors said, how's she doing?'

'They're hoping she'll be conscious soon. They wanted her body to take its time to recover. For a few minutes, last night, Bec, I thought I'd lose her forever.' He sobbed the last few words. His shoulders heaved as he covered his face with his palms and cried.

She hugged him and cried too. After a few minutes, she looked over to Puja's parents – they seemed a little more collected, and she sensed it was ok to approach them now. Mrs Khan looked up at her in astonishment. 'Oh, my God, Bec, you're here? When did you arrive?'

Tearfully, she hugged Rebecca, who whispered soothing words about Puja being strong and will recover from this.

Mr Khan, now back from what looked like a coffee run, was also surprised and happy to see Rebecca. He said, in a quiet voice, whilst putting the disposable coffee cups on the table, 'My Puja nearly died, Bec!'

Through her tears, Rebecca said, 'Mr Khan, she is the bravest person ever. She will be ok. Don't worry, we are all here for her.'

And then Molly spoke up, 'I'll be here for as long as you require me to be.'

They looked at her in dismay, Rebecca had forgotten she was even there. She held her gaze on Molly, who then said, 'Hey Beckie, how are you? Not seen you in ages.' She smiled at Rebecca sweetly.

She hated Molly calling her that. Rebecca again wondered what had possessed Samuel to call her. Her eyes narrowed as she studied Molly, who was dressed in torn jeans and a black cotton top that had the words '*Not your Honey*' printed in silver. Her hair was uncombed, she looked a mess, as if she'd arrived after a night out.

Rebecca replied curtly, 'Apart from my best friend nearly dying, I'm fine. And please don't call me Beckie, it's Rebecca or Bec.'

Molly gave a stifled laugh, 'Yeah, sure, *Rebecca*!' She emphasised.

Rebecca was in no mood for Molly's games. So she muttered an excuse to the Khan's about going to check on Samuel. But after Rebecca had sat down next to Samuel, Molly sidled over. Samuel said nothing to either of them. He stared at the floor in front of him as if in a trance.

Molly turned to Rebecca, 'So I hear congrats are in order.'

Rebecca glared at her, 'Yes, thanks, who told you?'

'Matt did.'

'My Matt? When did you see him?'

'Last night,' she giggled. 'He was pretty drunk and merry, if you know what I mean.'

'Matt was with you? I texted him and he didn't reply!' she said frowning.

'*Your Matt* was drunk, plus he'd left his phone at home. Maybe he wanted to run away from his needy soon-to-be wife!' She grinned and tried to make it sound like a joke. Rebecca already didn't like Molly, so this attempt at disguising a jibe with humour was not appreciated.

'The two of you went out alone?' Her voice dropped to a whisper.

Molly answered, with a huge smile and her sweetest voice, 'Of course not, there were a few, fifty, or sixty people there.'

Rebecca wanted to scream at her, why was she being so obtuse? But she stayed calm for Puja's sake. She responded in the same manner, with a smile and her nicest voice, 'Well I'm glad you both had a good time, he needs a bit of fun at the moment.' Then she stood up to speak to Puja's parents.

After nearly an hour of waiting, the doctor came out to tell them that Puja had regained consciousness and was responding well to treatment. The doctor also said she would make a full recovery.

Rebecca sighed and looked over at Samuel who put his head in his hands and moaned, Puja's parents, she noticed, had not spoken to him. She supposed they were blaming him for what had happened to their daughter.

Whilst Mr and Mrs Khan went in to see her, Molly took her leave, saying she was glad Puja was ok and may come back later to visit. Rebecca was glad to see the back of her. She had noticed Molly looking more and more tired as the morning had worn on. Probably the hard night of partying with Matt the previous night, she thought grimly.

Once Rebecca was alone with Samuel, she asked him why he'd called Molly to the hospital, but he said he hadn't. 'Bec I tried you several times, I knew you'd want to be here, but when I couldn't get a hold of you, I tried Matt, who didn't pick up at first either. Then Molly must have got a hold of his phone, and she said she'd call you and come straight away. She rang off before I could tell her not to come. So, when she got here, I couldn't turn her away! It wasn't the time for one of her dramas.'

Rebecca nodded and said it was ok – Molly squeezed herself into a lot of places she didn't need to be, and for the sake of Puja's parent's, Samuel had been right not to ask her to leave. She knew Molly was annoying, but to lie and say Matt left his phone at home whilst she still had access to it was underhand!

When Rebecca and Samuel finally got to see Puja, she looked drained, so Rebecca only stayed a few minutes. Samuel urged her to go home as there was nothing more she could do, anyway. She protested, but he told her he was fine the moment he knew Puja was on the mend. Puja's parents were also starting to thaw towards him, now they knew he had done his best the night before.

Knowing Puja's parents wouldn't be hostile to Samuel anymore, she agreed to go home. It was nearly one o'clock, and she was hungry. In the taxi she looked at her phone and noticed a few messages from her parents, asking how Puja was, but still nothing from Matt. She expected he was sleeping off his hangover. She had already reached out to him, he now had to make the next move, she wasn't going to beg.

Rebecca texted Frank on Monday for the first time after his fight with Matt and asked for a week off. She apologised for giving him such short notice and explained about Puja's close shave with death. He texted back saying ok – that was it, and although she was surprised, she was also glad. She knew she would have one hell of a conversation with him when they did get a chance to meet. But for now, they needed time to consider their positions.

Over the next few days, Rebecca visited Puja several times at home. Her parents had insisted she move back so they could keep an eye on her. She called on Samuel too and began worrying about him. He was missing his girlfriend. He'd spent an hour or two at her parent's house, but he told Rebecca he just wanted her back home, at their flat.

Rebecca finally heard from Matt that Sunday, after his Friday night out with Molly. He was nonchalant about their evening. He said he thought nothing was wrong with them spending time together. She remembered Molly had been Matt's friend since long before Rebecca had known her. Their friendship changed as soon as she had got together with Matt. Molly's comments towards her became sarcastic, and eventually, Rebecca made sure they saw her as little as possible. She invited only Puja and Samuel to their nights out. Rebecca confided in Puja about Molly's jealousy towards her, and when Puja agreed, Rebecca knew she wasn't imagining it. Matt just thought Rebecca was reading too much into it.

But since Macy's funeral, Rebecca noticed that Molly had been texting Matt more than usual. Rebecca was sure he'd confided in her regarding their recent problems including the altercation with Frank. To hell with her, she thought.

Samuel told her that the restaurant had investigated the incident and couldn't understand how Puja's food had become contaminated. The doctors verified that the nuts she'd consumed that night were likely to be due to a lot more than accidental cross-contamination. They confirmed that even the normal foods the restaurant served didn't contain ingredients that would cause such a reaction. Samuel and the Khan's were baffled. But whatever had happened that night, they were all glad that Puja was ok and learned a valuable lesson about the consequences of not taking her EpiPen.

Rebecca's new concerns were saving her relationship with Matt and smoothing her position at work. She needed to talk to Frank. She hadn't texted him on his private mobile phone number in a long time, but she wanted to see him away from prying eyes.

"Hi, Frank, it's Rebecca. Hope you are well, I'm sure you didn't expect me to contact you like this, I'm sorry if it's an inconvenience, but after your impromptu call on Matt, I guess we need to speak privately and hope you don't mind me texting. I think clearing the air before I get back from leave would be the best thing for all of us to do, look forward to hearing from you. Thanks, Rebecca."

She sent the message, if she hadn't sent it then, she wouldn't have done it at all. Within a few minutes, she got a reply.

"Hi Frey, yes I am well, thanks. I agree we

*should speak soon. Can you meet with me on
Sunday evening? That way I can clarify what
happened between Matt and I before you return
to work on Monday. If that is an unsuitable time,
please choose a date and time you
prefer. Frank."*

'Curt,' she thought. He'd called her 'Frey' too, when
they were casually dating, just like her father did. At
work, he only called her by her proper name. Yet, here
he was, calling her Frey again. She smiled, replying that
Sunday evening was fine, and she agreed to meet him at
the Starbucks near their office. It was equidistant from
both their homes, but he replied that he preferred it if
she came to his apartment instead, and he offered to
cook dinner.

Rebecca wasn't sure if going to his place for dinner
was appropriate, but despite her reservations, she
accepted his invitation.

On the last few days of her leave from work,
she spent more time with Matt. She was there more
often, they had gone to see a movie, had dinner out
twice and watched Netflix programmes. Although she
still loved Matt, she could tell something was missing,
and she knew it wasn't from her lack of trying. Sometimes, he pushed her away from him, and Molly's
involvement in Matt's life was palpable. He mentioned
things that Molly had suggested, or giggled about something funny she'd said. Rebecca smiled when he
mentioned her but secretly, she hated hearing these

stories. She said nothing to Matt in case they had an argument – she didn't want that.

For a Sunday outing, Matt suggested they go to Brighton for the day, but Rebecca refused, saying she needed to prepare for work on Monday, and she wanted to spend the whole day at home, getting her head together.

On Saturday night, whilst she was with Matt, she got a message from Frank to confirm she was still coming over the next day – he wanted to cook steak for dinner. Matt didn't see the notification when it came up on her phone. She made an excuse to go to the toilet and texted him back to confirm. He'd 'remembered' that steak was one of her favourite foods!

The next day, she picked out her A-line denim skirt, a light blue knitted jumper with tiny white flowers embroidered all over it, tights and boots to wear later in the evening. When it was time to get ready, she carefully combed her hair, applied subtle make-up and put on the clothes she'd chosen earlier.

She wanted to leave quietly, so her parents wouldn't question her too much, but Erin smiled when she came downstairs. 'Darling, you look lovely.' Rebecca busied herself, saying a quick 'thanks, Mum' before dashing out. Then she heard her mother shout after her, 'Tell Matt I said hi, and invite him over for dinner next week. I'll cook something nice.'

Rebecca didn't respond, she just waved back and drove off. It took thirty minutes to get to Frank's apartment. She became steadily more nervous as she got closer, but she kept her cool. She wasn't a teenager doing anything illegal! Well, that's what she told herself as she entered the lift to his apartment.

Frank opened the door immediately. 'Hey, Frey, thanks for coming.' She smiled and mumbled something back and walked in. He suggested they have a cocktail he'd made up for her visit, insisting it tasted amazing. His apartment had changed since she'd been there last. It was decorated in grey and silver tones. He had good taste in home décor, if nothing else. She noticed he had a few new pieces of art, some sculptures, at least two new pigment watercolour paintings and a modern chandelier that looked perfect in this setting.

As Frank was busying himself, talking to her about his day, she stole a look at him from the corner of her eyes. Damn, he looks sexy, she reflected, her heart rate quickened, and she took long, deep breaths to calm herself. He was wearing a baby-blue tee-shirt and faded jeans. He had nothing on his feet. She remembered him saying he preferred to go barefoot when he was at home. Nothing he wore was over the top, yet she thought he looked dashing tonight.

'So, what do you think, a good idea right?' he was asking.

She had zoned out, watching him talk, so she didn't know what he was asking her. She admitted she had not heard his question. 'Sorry I was miles away, what did you say again?'

'I said, let's talk first then have dinner on my

balcony. Don't worry, I have outdoor heaters.' He flashed her a big smile.

'Yeah, that sounds great.'

'Ok, good, now here is your cocktail.'

'Thank you.' Taking the glass from him she saw the liquid was red, she sipped it gingerly. 'Hmmm nice, what is it?'

He was watching for her reaction, he wanted to wow her with his cocktail 'Well… obviously, I can't say. It's a secret Pearson recipe!' He threw his head back and laughed.

She giggled. 'Very funny' *God, he looks good when he laughs*, and from this proximity, she could smell his musky aftershave. She needed to behave, she had to be businesslike and focus on why she was here, so she glanced away, saying, 'So, when do we discuss what happened with you and Matt?'

His smile faded, and she felt guilty for bringing the subject up.

'Yes sure,' he said. 'Ok, let me start first.' He sat on the sofa opposite her. 'Before I begin, I'd like to thank you for giving me an opportunity to speak freely.'

She nodded, to show she understood. Frank was glad he'd poured his heart out to his uncle when he'd come down from Scotland to see him. Now that his uncle had gone back, he'd called him to get advice for when he met with Rebecca. It was that advice he would put into motion today.

He continued, 'I'll start from the beginning and tell you some things you may already know.' He drew a deep breath. 'When we first stopped seeing each other, I found it a difficult to deal with. I took time off work, and when I returned, I worked in our Scottish office for a while. All this was good for me and helped me work through my feelings towards you.

'When I got back from Scotland and worked with you again, it helped knowing you had moved on and found a new boyfriend. That let me know there was no hope for me. I like working with you and you are a good employee – I was glad of the new, professional relationship we built up.

'Over the past two years, I've become reliant on your continued support at work and as a friend. You've never referred to our past involvement or made me uncomfortable by discussing you and Matt, and I appreciate that.

'But I guess whenever I heard anyone discussing you two, it seemed to me as if you both had – pardon me for saying it – a bit of an immature relationship.'

She raised her eyebrows at that. He gave her an apologetic smile then hurriedly said, 'Well not because of you. I know what you're like, but I did detect a slight change in you. You're a bit silly sometimes, and you've started behaving rather childlike, to match Matt, I'm sure. But despite that, you were happy and that made me glad.

'However, when Matt's mother passed away, I saw a different side to you at work, you didn't look your usual self. And then I overheard you saying to someone that Matt was blanking you, and it was upsetting you.

Frankly, I was seeing your relationship turn for the worse, and I felt helpless.

'I knew I was the last person to be offering you a shoulder to cry on. It would have looked creepy in everyone's eyes, including mine. So, I had to just stand on the sidelines and watch you go through it without my support.

'But when I found out you'd got engaged, I lost it. I couldn't believe he would propose and that you'd accept. I assume the death of his mother has forced his hand, somehow. Her demise will have mixed his emotions up, and although you suspected something was wrong, you didn't want to refuse him because you felt obligated or sorry for him.

'So, I wanted to reason with him and find out if his motives were genuine and just advise him in a friendly way, not to rush into a marriage until the dust had settled following his mother's death. But everything went wrong when I got there. He was aggressive, rude and didn't even want to listen.

'To be honest, I can see his point of view. I was your last romantic interest, giving him life tips. What gave me the right to do that? I understand that, yet we both have your best interests at heart, and that's the point. But he wouldn't listen to anything I said.

'I want you to know I didn't go there with the intention to start an argument. And I'd like to apologise to both of you if I have caused any problems. I hope you will understand.' He finished with a deep sigh.

Rebecca silently listened to his explanations, when

he put it like that, it all made sense. Yet she wished this conversation hadn't been necessary in the first place. She too, was happy things had settled between Frank and her. But as she thought about it, she became aware of buried feelings bubbling to the surface.

'Thanks for explaining it, and I'm glad you now know you were wrong to visit Matt that day, or any day. But from my point of view, I think what Matt did was wrong too, and I'd like to apologise on his behalf. To be honest Frank, I wish we weren't here talking about this at all. I love working at Crofts and Castles – I don't want this to affect my job.' She looked up to see his reaction.

His heart skipped a beat, he wished she wouldn't gaze at him like that. Her eyes fixed on him, whilst her pink lips, which had a touch of lip-gloss, were slightly parted. He looked away hastily saying, 'Frey, there is nothing that could affect your job. Plus, you did nothing wrong. Everything that happened was because I was foolish. I wasn't thinking as clearly as I should have been.'

He looked downtrodden, she then put him out of his misery. 'Ok, let's draw a line under this silly episode and move on.'

He gave her a huge smile that made her heart quicken again. '*For God's sake, you're engaged to Matt, so behave,*' she scolded herself. She smiled back.

'I'm so glad we sorted it out, you are a gem. I hope you know that.' Without waiting for a reply, he said, 'So shall I make a start on those juicy steaks?

Trust me, you will love it.' He stood up, still looking at her.

She got up too, 'Yeah, let me help you.'

'Don't be silly, I'm the host, and you're the guest.'

She laughed, 'You're so kind, ok, let me talk to you in the kitchen. That way, I'm already there if you need me to get my hands dirty.'

He relented, 'Ok, fine. You can tell me all the details about your friend Puja, and her brush with death.'

They walked to the kitchen to prepare dinner. Rebecca recited the whole episode of what happened last weekend. He was attentive and interested in all she had to say.

She listened to what he'd done when his uncle had come over and the general gossip from work this last week while she'd been on holiday. Rebecca didn't notice the time flying, and before she knew it, it was midnight. She'd had a lovely evening with him, and there had been no awkwardness, apart from the first part of the evening. She had also asked him to keep their meeting a secret from work and their families for obvious reasons. Rebecca couldn't wait to speak to Puja about tonight, she was the only person she would share it with.

After she had gone, Frank closed the door and walked to his balcony to watch her drive away. As her car disappeared from view, he stared out into the night air, which was now cold and fresh. He was glad things had gone well tonight.

Rebecca had opened up towards him, which was

something she'd not done before. Was she interested in him again? No, she couldn't be, she was engaged to Matt. He continued debating with himself for a further few minutes out in the cold. Then he took himself inside and decided tonight had been a success.

Rebecca was happy with him and he was thrilled that she wouldn't have to leave the company because of what had happened. Frank was glad he would see her tomorrow, but he felt it was too long to wait! He had to be careful, he needed to stay professional at work. Frank resolved that when he had the time, he would speak to his uncle about tonight's meeting.

Over the next month, things settled down at work and with Matt. They were having fewer arguments. Rebecca gave Puja all the details of her meeting with Frank, and they speculated about Frank's feelings for her. She confessed to enjoying her time with Frank, and for a few days after, Puja kept ringing her, asking how things were going between her and Frank, but there was nothing to tell. They had kept their relationship formal, both holding onto their side of the deal.

In the second month of her engagement to Matt, and on a Monday afternoon, Frank called her into the office. He looked serious. Rebecca worried she had displeased him. He didn't even crack a smile, which was what he did to ease the tension.

Her palms began sweating and she nervously rubbed

them on the side of her pants, he closed the door and the blinds. He wanted utmost discretion.

'What's the matter, Frank? Did I do something wrong?' she asked, eyebrows furrowed, and her lips pressed together in anticipation.

'Can you take a seat please, Frey?' he asked.

He never called her Frey in the office, 'Frank?'

'Please, can you sit down?' he commanded.

She did as directed. He came near her, and crouching beside her, he said, 'Frey, I got a personal phone call just now and I have some upsetting news.'

'What?'

'Just know I will be there for you, no matter what, ok?'

'Frank, please, what is it?' she begged.

'Frey, your mum just called me. She said she couldn't talk to you, so she asked if I would speak to you instead.'

'My mum? She has my mobile number! Why do you need to get involved?'

Taking a deep breath in, and with pity in his eyes, he said, 'Frey, your dad has just passed away. He had a heart attack.'

Rebecca stared at him in confusion, he was talking rubbish. She had seen her father this morning, and he'd been fine! The room spun, she felt sick. She wanted to say something but couldn't. Everything suddenly blacked out.

6

The phone call Frank received from Rebecca's mother stunned him. He looked over at her, and his heart broke. He guessed Erin had been unable to tell Rebecca such devastating news, and knowing that he was always supportive of her, she had asked him to break the news on her behalf.

When Rebecca fainted, he felt helpless and didn't know what to do, so he held her in his arms for a while. He wanted her to stay that way for as long as she could so she didn't have to deal with reality. When she finally came around, she was groggy and couldn't understand where she was and why Frank was with her; he had to tell her again.

She screamed first, then howled and then cried. At that, the other staff came running into the office. Frank had to explain that she had found out her father had passed away, and she needed space to grieve.

They looked at Rebecca sadly. Lisa, the accountant,

cried and backed away from the office. After a little time, Frank escorted Rebecca into his car to drive her to the hospital to meet with her mother and see her father. She was in a daze and wept for most of the journey.

When they got there, they made their way to the mortuary, Erin was sitting outside the room where Finn's body lay. She didn't pay them any attention – even when Frank spoke to her, she said nothing.

He placed Rebecca, who was still crying, on the chair next to Erin and whispered, 'Mrs Reid, Erin, it's me, Frank.' He was getting worried, looking at them. One was crying, and the other sitting there staring into oblivion.

She acknowledged him at last, 'Frank, what are you doing here? Finn is in there, waiting for Rebecca.'

He took a deep breath in, then he spoke gently as if addressing a small child, 'Yes, Mrs Reid. Rebecca is here beside you, I will take her in, ok?'

Erin smiled, 'Frank I always considered you a good friend to my daughter, she is so lucky to have you.'

He dismissed her comments and looked at Rebecca, who had now stopped weeping, it was her turn to zone out. Then he heard the double doors open, and Matt came running to her. Rebecca, on seeing him, got up and ran the little distance into his arms, crying, 'My dad is gone Matt, he left me!'

Frank watched them and felt a stab of pain. He wanted to support her like Matt could right now, but he had to keep his feelings in check – this wasn't the time for him to be selfish.

'What happened, Bec?' Matt asked as he held her. His eyes scanned the area behind her, he saw Frank looking concerned. He flashed him a look of contempt and asked her, 'They told me Finn is inside, are you ready to see him?' He looked at the door opposite them.

She nodded a 'yes'.

They called a member of staff who could allow Rebecca into the room. Frank watched them enter, his heart heavy, and as soon as he heard her cry from inside, his legs gave way. He sat next to Erin, put his palms on his face and forced himself not to cry. He had never felt this helpless.

R ebecca couldn't remember many of the events after her father's death. Everything was a blur, from Frank telling her the news in the office, her visit to the hospital mortuary, Matt looking after her, Puja visiting her, everything. She was just going through the motions in a daze.

She couldn't understand how her healthy, happy father was here one day then gone the next. It made no sense. Matt was being supportive, and her house had become a hive of constant activity. The old couple next door, Mr and Mrs Crowe were always over, making cups of tea and bringing over home-cooked food. But even their little dog Lucy, who always made Rebecca smile, could not get one out of her now.

To Rebecca's annoyance, Molly was also there, trying to support them. She was a dark shadow that followed Matt everywhere, and he was oblivious to it. Puja did her bit to make Molly uncomfortable, but it didn't make any difference. Molly wanted to be around Matt. Rebecca was in no mood to say anything.

Frank came round too, mostly late at night when everyone else had gone. He stayed with Erin and Rebecca, talking to them about their day. He even updated her on gossip at work to take her mind away from her loss. Erin came out of her shell a lot more. She even laughed now and again.

Frank didn't want to run into Matt in the daytime, so he preferred to meet her this way, at home, after everyone had gone. They all kept his late-night drop-ins a secret, it wasn't agreed, just assumed. Rebecca looked forward to his visits. Sometimes she saved her inner-most feelings from Matt so she could share them with Frank later.

Rebecca tried talking to Matt about it, but all he kept saying was that it would get easier. Every time she mentioned something on her mind about her father, he kept repeating, in different ways, that in time it will fade. But Frank, he understood, he nodded his head and listened. He laughed with her when she relived a joke she shared with her father. He was just easier to talk to.

Frank said he wanted to take care of the funeral costs.

Rebecca and Erin protested and told him it wasn't necessary. Erin said she had savings, and Finn had been sensible with money, but Frank would not take no for an answer. He wanted to do something meaningful and feel less helpless by organising the funeral. Rebecca worried about how Matt would take it if he found out about Frank's generous offer. Erin hastily added, 'Who gives a crap what he thinks?'

Frank suppressed a smile. Erin had always supported his relationship with Rebecca, but Finn had been harder to please when they were dating.

Rebecca exploded, 'He is my fiancé Mum, how can you say that?'

'Easily, he is just an immature child. And I don't like the fact he's your fiancé!' she snapped.

Rebecca's face reddened, her nostrils flared, and she opened her mouth to speak, but Frank intervened.

'Now, now ladies! If I knew you would fight about me, I would have brought over boxing gloves! Come on, be nice. This isn't the time for arguments.' He tried his best to calm them with his little joke.

They stared at each other for a second. What's the point in reasoning with her,' Rebecca seethed, 'she's as cold as an ice queen!'

Her mum turned on her heels and went upstairs. Over her shoulder, she said, 'Goodnight Frank, please talk some sense into her. I'll see you tomorrow night, won't I?'

'Yes, you will, Mrs Reid,' he half-yelled, to make sure his voice travelled up the stairs.

Still scowling, Rebecca whispered under her breath, 'She gets away with murder!'

'Frey, don't be like that, she's lost her husband.'

'And I've lost my father, that's harder!' she said sulkily.

'This isn't a competition of who is finding this more difficult Frey, you both are. Now come on, let us open a bottle of wine and let our hair down.' He smiled, trying to take her focus from her mother, whilst making his way over to the wine rack.

Smiling back, she said, 'I'm not a kid you can bribe with alcohol!'

'Do you want a glass or not? You know it will relax you.' He grinned.

She was glad he was with her, she smirked and nodded her head in acceptance.

Whilst he was opening the wine, he said, 'You will be busy anyway, helping me with the arrangements, choosing the floral preferences, organising the eulogy, the newspaper announcement…' he trailed off.

He turned around as soon as he heard a sob, Rebecca was crying again. He rushed over to soothe her. She was slumped over the breakfast bar. He could do nothing more than hold her. There were no words.

Rebecca lapped up the attention Frank gave her whilst she was grieving, he was the only ray of sunshine she had. She talked to Puja about him and expressed her concerns. She didn't want anyone to think she was cheating on Matt, after all, her friendship with him was innocent.

Puja listened but was honest with her, 'You aren't cheating on Matt, but it won't please him if he ever finds out Frank is spending time with you this way, even if it is innocent. For God's sake Rebecca, you are dealing with a bereavement. You do whatever it takes, get the support you need from whoever gives it to you the best.'

Rebecca raised her eyebrows, she giggled, '"*Gives it to me the best*"? You sure have a way with words, babe.'

Puja laughed, 'Sorry, I didn't mean it that way!'

They changed the subject. Rebecca also told her she was anxious about Frank wanting to pay for the funeral. He could afford it, but she didn't want to take advantage of him or risk Matt finding out and going nuts. Puja disagreed, 'Babe, Frank is trying to help the two of you. Let him. He cares for you, and the last thing he wants you to do right now, is worry about money.'

'We aren't poor.'

'You aren't, but I think Frank feels helpless. Rebecca, you must see, he's in love with you. There's Matt buzzing around you like a dazed bee, and he wants to be the one doing that instead but can't. This way, at least he can do something helpful.'

'I agree with everything you said, apart from the "*in love with me*" part! Sometimes, Puja, you have an over-active imagination.' She smiled.

'I'm just calling it as I see it, Bec.'

'Hmm, I still think you're wrong.'

'Disagree all you want, but I have eyes, and I use them.' She said, smiling.

'And you've got legs, so use them and make me a cup of tea!' Rebecca laughed at her.

Puja slapped Rebecca's hand, 'You slave driver!' and headed towards the kitchen smiling.

In the days following the tragedy, Rebecca had been reluctant to leave the house. She was still licking her wounds, and nobody could force her to go out till she was ready. As she thought on this she recalled how Matt had been when his mum died. He had stayed at home like a hermit for weeks.

A few days later, Frank called Rebecca, 'Hey Frey, I've started the funeral plans. I rang the hospital and found out that your dad's body is with the coroners. I need a release date for the funeral directors, but they told me they can't give me one.'

Rebecca frowned, 'Did you ask them if they needed a member of the family to sign something?'

He sighed, 'No I didn't, but I got the impression they will not be forthcoming.'

'That's strange, when Matt's mother died, they kept her for longer for the forensic pathologist. My dad had a heart attack, there shouldn't be a problem with releasing him.'

'Or could it be because he'd been dead for longer six hours? They may have to rule out other things.' Frank was struggling to make sense of it.

'I don't understand it, and please don't speak to my

mother about it. Do you want me to do anything to help?'

'No, you relax, let me make a few phone calls first.'

'Relax?'

He hastily added, 'Yes, as best you can under the circumstances.'

'Ok, call me when you have more news.'

He promised he would and rang off.

That evening, he arrived for his usual late-night visit. When he was sure Erin wasn't listening, he said, 'Sorry Frey, they won't tell me anything or give me a release date.' He shrugged his shoulders.

'Maybe it's because you're not family. Let me try tomorrow, give me the numbers to call.'

'Ok, but I doubt you will get answers. They never even asked if I was family. They just kept saying they didn't have a release date to give me.'

She reflected on what he said. It sounded odd. She studied Frank – today, he was wearing a light-blue hoodie, black Levi jeans and a black pair of Nike trainers. He dressed in informal clothes when he came over, it was strange to see. She was so used to him wearing formal clothes in the office. He looked much younger than his thirty-two years in casual clothes.

She tried not to notice how sexy he was, to stay aloof – but he was making it difficult for her to do that. It was becoming harder and harder for her to ignore the tug of the old chemistry that seemed to be resurfacing between them. There wasn't much she could do to control it either. Was it just her, or did he feel it too?

Detective Chief Inspector Christopher Mills of the London Metropolitan Police was young and ambitious. He was a tall man with broad shoulders, he had a face that rarely broke into a smile, but when he did, he showed his perfectly white teeth that celebrities paid a high price for. His light brown hair was perfectly combed; he took pride in his appearance.

He was tasked to investigate the case of Mr Finn Reid. Nearly all he knew about the deceased and his family was normal. He hated being given open-and-shut cases. He wanted something meaty he could get into and work with, but his detective superintendent had promised him that as soon as he'd wrapped this case up, he would give him something more exciting.

Everything he'd achieved, he credited to hard work. His job entailed intense scrutiny and a high workload, but he didn't complain – he was single and happy to work all the hours they gave him because he loved the job so much.

He'd joined the police service at twenty-eight, and within two years of finishing his detective training, he'd made the rank of detective.

They had paired him with Detective Sargent Xavier Townsend for this case. Townsend was a foot shorter than him, he adopted a fashionable reddish brown beard that was well groomed and kept at medium length. His eyes were cornflower blue, and he had laughter lines around them that authenticated his cheerful nature. He approved of Townsend, who had just finished his detective training and was still in consolidation mode. Townsend came to introduce himself. Mills noticed he was neatly turned out and polite. He seemed highly observant and incisive too. Townsend missed little and was popular with his colleagues. He was the type of man, Mills felt, you'd want to have covering your back, if needed.

'Townsend, what brings you here?' he asked, flashing him his big Hollywood smile.

'Very funny, work and Mr Finn Reid's case. Shall we get this show on the road? They inform me it's an open-and-shut case.'

'You and me both Townsend, nothing like ticking boxes to assure them we have done our duty eh? Come on, let's go, I've had an update from the coroner's office, I'll brief you on the way over.' he said, standing up, taking his jacket from behind his chair and walking towards the exit, making Townsend rush to keep up with him.

They got into Mills' unmarked car and drove to the Reids' house. When they arrived at the crescent-shaped close, they searched for the house. They slowed to a crawl as they peered out at the house numbers. Townsend pointed to the right. 'Twenty-two – over there,' he said.

The Reids' house was a detached property with a manicured lawn, a garage to the left and a little Fiat on the drive. Mills guessed it belonged to their only daughter. It was a light powder blue, like a cloudless sky.

The detectives climbed out of the car and walked up to the front door. Townsend pressed the doorbell. After waiting a while, he pressed it again. Moments after the second ring, he heard a woman's voice say, 'Ok, hang on, hang on. I'm nearly there.'

Someone opened the door, but nobody greeted them, the lady left it opened and walked away. They glanced at each other in surprise then stepped inside, Mills gave a little cough and said, 'Mrs Reid?'

Erin spun around in shock. They saw a well groomed, attractive woman with red hair tied into a ponytail at the nape of her neck, tendrils of her loose hair framed her face. She wore a blue dressing gown which she clutched tighter around her when she saw the two men.

Detective Mills reassured her, 'Don't be alarmed, Mrs Reid, I'm Detective Chief Inspector Christopher Mills, and my colleague here is Detective Sergeant Xavier Townsend. We need to ask you a few questions, if that's ok.'

Erin sighed apologetically, 'I am so sorry, Detectives, I assumed you were my daughter's fiancé, he was due to visit us this morning. Since my husband's death, he has become a regular to our house, so I opened the door thinking it was him. Do come in and shut the door. Would you like a seat?' She pointed to the sofa. 'If I'd known I was having guests, I would have dressed up.' She was still clutching her dressing gown. She clearly didn't want them to see her this state.

'Don't worry, Mrs Reid,' Townsend said. 'It's our fault for visiting unannounced.'

Erin smiled and led them into her living room.

As the two detectives ventured further into the house, Mills looked around. There was a beautiful marble fireplace with carefully placed family photos on the mantelpiece and an ornate silver mirror above it. The sofas were covered in cream leather. There was a glass coffee table on the mushroom-coloured plush rug. Looking around him, he could see the family took pride in their house. Everything seemed in place. Almost as if they were expecting visitors, it looked more like a show home than one that was lived in.

After taking a seat, Erin asked, 'Would you like a cup of tea or coffee?'

'We are fine Mrs Reid, thank you. Is your daughter around? We need to talk to her too,' replied Detective Mills.

Erin's eyes narrowed and she looked at them with concern. 'Is everything all right, Detectives? Has something happened?'

'No, but we have routine questions, and if we speak to you both together, it will save time.' Mills did his best to put her at ease.

She gave him a half-smile and said, 'Ok, Detective, yes, she is upstairs. I will fetch her. Please give me a minute.'

The two detectives smiled at her. She hurried up the stairs. They heard nothing for a while then Erin came back. She said, 'She will be here in a minute.'

'Thank you, Mrs Reid. This is a nice place, have you lived here long?' asked Detective Townsend.

She smiled and looked around her home. 'Yes, it is, I like it. We have lived here since Rebecca was a child. We have refurbished it several times. It needs constant maintenance. You know what houses are like, something or other always needs updating.'

Just then, Rebecca appeared. She had the same hair colour as her mother, but she had a lot of it and it tumbled down her back. She was wearing a grey tee-shirt and black tracksuit bottoms. On her feet, she had fluffy grey bootie slippers. At first, she stared at them with a slight frown on her face, then she forced a smile.

Both the detectives stood up, and Mills said, 'Hello, you're Rebecca, I take it. We need to ask you both a few questions.'

She answered, 'Yes, sure, Detective, please take a seat.'

When they were all settled, Rebecca said, 'Has this got something to do with my dad's release date?'

The detectives looked at each other, Mills answered, 'I'm not sure, have you been trying to get one from the coroner's office?'

'Yes, we tried, but they haven't been forthcoming.' Rebecca said, pushing a lock of stray hair behind her ear.

Erin said, 'You never mentioned this. We will need to bury your dad soon. Shall I ring them and find out? You shouldn't worry about this, I'm your mother and his wife…' she stopped then corrected herself, '… well was his wife.'

'It's fine Mum, Frank and I will sort it out. Anyway Detectives, maybe you might help now you are here.' She looked at them.

Mills was watching them as they talked and noticed a distance between them. Grief does strange things to people. He said, 'Actually ladies, we have a reason Mr Reid is still under the coroner's jurisdiction. When they examined him, they found bruises around his wrists.'

Both the Reid women glanced at each other, then Erin asked, 'What do you mean?'

Mills answered her, 'When Mr Reid was found, they assumed he'd had a heart attack. His pacemaker had been replaced nine years ago, the paramedics and doctors both agreed it was the heart attack that killed him. However, upon further examination, they noticed signs of bruising to his arm, they transferred Mr Reid from the hospital morgue to the coroner's morgue for further investigation. We want to find out why Mr Reid had this bruising on his wrist. It also left fingernail impressions. There's most likely a simple explanation, but we have to check this out before we can be clear to release him.'

Both women were silent for a few moments. Then Erin asked her daughter, 'Did you play fight with your dad the day he died? You both mess around sometimes.'

Rebecca frowned deep in thought, 'Not really, Mum, I saw him in the morning, before I went to work. The night before, I wasn't at home, so no, I didn't. Could you have?'

It was Erin's turn to think, then she said she couldn't have caused it either. He'd died on a Monday morning, so he'd not been to work, neither had he been out of the house much that weekend. She asked, 'I don't understand it, is it a big deal?'

Mills answered again, 'We like to make sure there are no suspicious circumstances. And if we're asked to look into something that seems strange, we are duty bound to investigate.'

'I understand Detective.' Erin replied.

Rebecca asked, 'If my dad had a slight bruise to his wrists, isn't that out of the ordinary? I can't imagine why he had those marks. If we are sure he didn't get them here, maybe he got them at work or outside that day?'

'We checked, Miss Reid. Your father hadn't been to work and his car was still in the garage. He hadn't left the house,' said Townsend.

Erin added, 'He was due to go into work on the later shift that day. So, he suffered the heart attack before going out.'

'That's correct, we wanted to find out if anyone could explain the bruising found around his wrist. The doctors still stand by their diagnosis that Mr Reid suffered a heart attack. His pacemaker had a sinus arrest which might have slowed Mr Reid's heart and caused it to stop. He may not have had time to even call for help.

His pacemaker wasn't working when they examined him.'

Rebecca started to cry, this was too much for her. Her mother put her arm around her.

Erin said, 'What does this mean? We need to wait for an explanation for the bruising before we can bury Finn?'

'We will check with the coroner and get back to you, Mrs Reid. Provided there is nothing else, we will take your leave,' said Detective Mills, standing up.

'So, what's the next step, Detectives?'

Detective Townsend said, 'Mrs Reid, we will go straight to the coroner's office now and when they have cleared Mr Reid's body for release, we will let you know.'

Erin forced a smile, 'Thank you, shall I see you out?'

'It's ok Mrs Reid, take care of Rebecca, we will see ourselves out.' Said Mills, ushering Townsend towards the front door.

The two detectives made their way to the coroner's office. They met with the assistant coroner, Mr Telford, a well-rounded man, who was looking stern. He said, 'Sorry, Detectives, but I have unfortunate news for you.'

'What is it?' Asked Mills.

'We will need to get consent from Mr Reid's family and conduct a post-mortem. He died three days ago, and time is of the essence.'

Detective Mills scratched his head, 'A post-mortem

for a few bruises? Surely we can release the body to the family?'

Mr Telford's tone was authoritative, 'Detective Mills, we have just discovered more than bruising to Mr Reid's body. We will need to have the post-mortem done right away. Our office has asked the family doctor to contact the Reid family to get consent.'

Detective Mills asked, 'What else did you discover, apart from the bruising?'

Mr Telford explained the reason for the post-mortem, they suspected foul play. Until they found out what had caused the heart attack, they couldn't release him for burial.

The two detectives rushed back to their car and drove immediately to the Reids' house. They were back fewer than two hours since their first visit. Mrs Reid opened the door. She didn't smile at them this time, but she invited them in anyway.

Rebecca was sitting in the living room with a young man who had his arm around her shoulder. When they entered the room, she looked up, her eyes red and puffy. The young man who was comforting her had brown hair and thick, bushy eyebrows.

The detectives introduced themselves, and he stated he was Rebecca's fiancé, Matt.

When they were all seated, Erin said, 'The doctor has just called to ask our permission to perform a post-mortem on my husband. You didn't tell us they would do that?' There was an edge to her voice.

'Mrs Reid, we didn't know ourselves until we got to the coroner's office.' Townsend said.

'Can you tell us why? You said it was bruising to the wrist, is that a good reason to do a post-mortem?' She frowned at them, stealing a look at a still sobbing Rebecca.

Detective Mills spoke, 'Mrs Reid we came here as soon as we found out. As far as we were aware, when we first got here this morning, your husband suffered a heart attack and had bruising on his wrist that he could have received quite innocently, and it wasn't suspicious. After meeting with the assistant coroner, he told us that Mr Reid had two puncture marks on his chest, under his heart. Which is why they want to investigate further.'

Matt thick eyebrows shot up, 'Puncture marks? Like a stabbing?'

Mills replied, 'Not really, the coroner suspects someone shot him with a stun gun. And if that's what happened, it could have caused his pacemaker to malfunction and fail.'

They were speechless, then a soft groan escaped from Rebecca, who had put her head up to listen to them speak. 'Who would want to kill my dad? This can't be happening!' she howled.

7

The detectives had gone ages ago, Rebecca lay on her bed. She couldn't cry anymore. Erin had taken everything in her stride and had even offered to make the detectives a cup of tea – after finding out someone had killed her husband! When the doctor arrived, she signed the consent for the post-mortem.

Matt was being kind to Rebecca at last. He, for once, didn't dismiss her out of hand, like he had been doing these last few days. Puja was over as soon as Matt called her. They attended to Erin and Rebecca all day. Mr and Mrs Crowe even visited with their dog Lucy, to see if there was anything they could do.

It was too much for Rebecca, the confusion and the commotion all day. But Erin appeared to be enjoying the extra attention, which made Rebecca even more fed up. By seven that evening, she asked them to leave – she'd had enough and needed to be alone.

Now, here she was, not crying, just lying on her bed, staring up at the ceiling. She asked, 'Who would want to kill my dad? And if they wanted something, like money or things from our house, why didn't they take it once they'd killed him? Does anything add up to you?'

From the corner of the room, where he was sitting on Rebecca's tub chair, Frank came over to sit beside her on her bed. She stared at him, glad he was there. He still looked handsome, even though his face appeared troubled.

'Frey, I told you to call me if you needed me. You don't have to go through this on your own.'

'I'm not on my own, they were all over here, but I didn't want them, they were buzzing around like a fly in my ear, speculating about what might have happened to my father. All I wanted was peace and quiet. I am so glad you're here Frank. If anyone can keep a lid on the chaos round here, you can.' She let out a deep sigh.

'Thanks Frey, I'm doing all I can. At least we now know why they wouldn't release his body. But I can't understand why someone would stun him with a gun?' He raked his fingers through his hair and stood up. He walked to the window, thinking of a reason, but couldn't come up with any.

Finally he said, 'So, let me get this straight. Finn didn't leave the house that day. At some point, somebody entered the house, restrained him with one hand and stunned him with the other. Right on his chest and through his clothes. That then affected his pacemaker, which killed him. Is that what happened?'

'That's what the detectives are saying.'

'So, when they had your dad's body, why didn't they find the marks the stun gun made?'

'I am not sure, Frank. I have a massive headache now, and I'm tired. There are too many questions and not enough answers.'

Frank studied her, she looked drained, her hair dishevelled. Her face was so pale, but her freckles were still visible, peppering her cheeks, nose and forehead, then his heart twisted with yearning. '*How beautiful she is, even amid such tragedy*,' he thought, 'I'm sorry Frey, I'll leave you alone. Get some rest.'

She asked in a soft voice, 'Frank, would it be inappropriate if I asked you to stay with me tonight?'

His eyebrows shot up in surprise. She saw she'd shocked him and quickly added, 'I just mean here, in my house, not in my bed, of course. It's nice to know you're around if I need you. I won't tell Matt. Am I asking too much?' Her face flushed in embarrassment.

He knew how easy it would be to say yes, knowing it wasn't right, he said, 'Frey, it's not a good idea. I could kip on your couch downstairs with no trouble, but what would your mum say? Plus, it might complicate things. If you prefer, I'll wait here with you till you sleep.' He desperately wanted to say yes, to snuggle into bed with her and hold her till she slept. She looked so inviting over there, so he looked away.

'You always say the right things. Yes please, can you stay until I fall asleep? I've got books you can read, on the bookshelf over there.' She pointed to it. 'I promise you I have normal books, not just chick-lit.' she grinned.

He looked at where she was pointing and then back at her. 'You're funny, and yes thanks, I will help myself. Let me make us something to drink. I will make a coffee for me, but maybe a glass of wine for you? You've had a long day, coffee will be no good for you to relax. A small glass of red?'

'Thanks Frank, that would be great.'

Once he'd returned to her room with the drinks, he tucked her into her sheets, propping her up on her pillow as she took a sip of her wine. He walked over to the bookshelf to browse, he turned around with a book in his hand, '*Fifty Shades of Grey?*' At first, he smirked, then he couldn't help himself and laughed out loud. 'My, my, Frey, you are a dark horse, aren't you?'

Once more she flushed, 'Put that back. Puja gave it to me, I haven't read it yet!'

'Let me see,' he flicked through the book and found a bookmark in the middle. 'Now Frey, I've found your place. Don't tell me you're not reading it,' he chuckled.

'Don't be silly, that's Puja's bookmark. I'm not ashamed. If I was reading it why would it be up there, on the shelf?'

'Ok, fine. Keep your knickers on! Literally!' he said and laughed, putting the book back.

She asked with a sly grin, 'Have *you* read it? You can borrow that copy! It's not on my reading list and since you are so interested, go right ahead!'

'No thanks, I prefer something that sets my heart

racing differently, like action and adventure or thriller books. I'm reading a brilliant one at the moment, really exciting – I can lend it to you if you like?'

'Nope, I prefer to get my adventure kicks from the movies or TV.'

'I love the way adventure books can take me around the world without actually leaving my home.' Walking closer to her bed, he said, 'Now, come on, put your glass down and get some sleep. You won't relax if your mind is on racy books, will you?' He was smiling and pleased his teasing had lightened her mood.

'Hmmm…' She put her glass on her bedside table and snuggled down. 'Night, Frank, thanks for staying.'

'Night Frey, sleep well.' He watched her find a comfortable position in which to sleep, he dared not get close to her, she was too tempting. He struggled to stay away from her as she slept just a few feet from him and fought the urge to tell her to dump that fool of a fiancé and be with him instead. Again, he reminded himself that this wasn't the time, he needed to be here for her whenever she asked, not satisfying his own agenda… yet!

Frank picked a non-fiction book from her bookshelf at random, it was a book about *The History of Scotland*, he smiled, Frey had to get her red hair from somewhere, and her Scottish heritage was just as good a place as any.

After reading a few pages and flicking through the book, stopping to read parts that appeared interesting, he glanced over at Rebecca, he could hear her. She was in deep sleep, she must have been so tired. He closed the book, put it on her dressing table and stood up to look at her again. She looked peaceful, he was glad she could forget her troubles for a few hours.

He left at ten-thirty, a lot earlier than he normally had over these past few days. He promised to call his uncle to give him an update – he knew that Logan didn't sleep early. He would call him as soon as he got into his car, via the Bluetooth hands-free, so when he got home, he could shower and jump into bed – he still had to go to work in the morning

There was a loud knock on Rebecca's door, her mother was shouting, 'Get up, it's ten o'clock. You can't sleep forever!' Erin banged the door once more then barged in.

Erin watched her daughter turn over to look at her. She rushed to the windows and threw the curtains wide open, letting light into the gloomy room and barked 'We've got to speak to the police soon. I stalled them till eleven, so get up and make yourself decent.' Not waiting for her to respond, she swept out of the room as quick as she'd come in.

Rebecca rubbed her eyes, yawned, then stretched over to her bedside table to get her phone. She grabbed it and dived back under the blankets, this time making sure her head was inside too. She wasn't ready for the day. Under the covers, she peered at her phone. There were messages from Matt, Puja and even one from Molly. She whispered, 'That conniving bitch!'

She was disappointed Frank hadn't messaged her, she didn't want him to think she was desperate, asking him to stay the night. What she'd asked for was innocent company, but what if he didn't think that? And had she been right to ask him to stay in the first place?

If anyone was needed to comfort her for the night, it should have been Matt – after all, he was her fiancé. And what would have happened if Matt found out Frank had stayed the night? It wouldn't be fair on either of the men. 'Bloody Frank!' she said out loud. Why does he have to be so sensible? She gave a big sigh, pushed her duvet off her and got out of bed. The light streaming in from the window was blinding, she needed to wake up and face the day. And then she remembered her father, her heart suddenly felt heavy, and sadness once again descended. She tried to brush the thoughts from her mind and went into her en-suite bathroom to run a bath.

When she came back out to wait for the bath to fill, she noticed the book Frank had left on her dressing table. She picked it up – *The History of Scotland*. She rifled through the first few pages, looking to see whose it was. She assumed it was Frank's, but she couldn't remember him coming in with a book. She knew it wasn't hers, so she made a mental note to ask him about it when she saw him later.

Once she was ready, had eaten breakfast and was waiting for the detectives, she texted Matt to tell him what was going on. He offered to come over straight away, he was out shopping with Molly and asked if he could bring her over too. Rebecca felt irritated, he never wanted to go shopping with her, but when Molly asked him, he happily followed her! 'No way,' she said out loud. That bitch was not coming anywhere near her. She texted a sweet reply to say it was kind of him, but she didn't need either of them.

Erin overheard her, 'What, love?'

Rebecca looked up from her phone, 'Sorry?'

'You said, "No way." Was that for me?' she asked, smiling.

'Oh, no, it was nothing. Just a random thing on my phone.' She didn't want to tell her mother about Matt and Molly. Erin clearly didn't like Matt, she wanted her daughter to dump him for Frank, but Rebecca didn't want to do whatever her mother asked of her. Even if she was right this time, damn it. Rebecca was trying to make sense of her feelings for both men. Following the death of their parents – Matt's mum and her father – she'd noticed a change in Matt. He wasn't the same man she'd fallen in love with.

Erin had gone back into the kitchen, Rebecca heard her mother put the radio on, and a few minutes later she was singing! She listened in disbelief, they'd learned that someone had murdered her dad only yesterday, his body was going through a post-mortem, and there she was singing! Talk about insensitive! She stormed over to the little radio in the kitchen and switched it off.

Erin looked at her, her face lost the smile she had and she began to scowl as she stopped dancing and singing. 'Rebecca, what's got into you? I was enjoying that.'

She took deep breaths in, her heart was racing, and her nostrils flared as she ranted, 'What's got into me? What the hell is wrong with you? Dad is on a cold metal table being cut open right now. Yesterday, we found out that his death wasn't any ordinary heart attack, and the detectives will be here soon. And you are dancing around like you're at a party! For God's sake Mum, if the detectives see you this way, you'll end up their number-one suspect!' She stared hard at her mother.

Erin said calmly. 'I see what you are saying. Ok, are you hungry? I want to make nibbles to eat later, and I need to have something to give the detectives when they come. We can't stop being human, let this terrible event change who we are.'

Rebecca felt deflated, her mother just didn't care, or she let nothing bother her. Now that she thought about it, she hadn't seen her cry much, either. She walked back to the living room to await the detectives.

Half an hour later, the two detectives had arrived, Detective Mills spoke, 'We can confirm that the marks found on Mr Finn Reid had been caused by a stun gun. It was near the heart, by his pacemaker. The post-mortem, which they did yesterday confirmed that the shock from the gun caused a massive heart attack. The suspect must have fired the gun for at least forty-five seconds to cause such damage.

'The assailant may have known he wore a pace-maker. We noticed there were no signs of a break-in, so

Mr Reid may well have known the person who attacked him. They found him inside the kitchen, so he must have invited the assailant in. If the attack had taken place by the front door, it would be less likely that Mr Reid would have known them.' He let that information sink in then said, 'Do you have any questions?'

Rebecca answered, 'Why didn't they spot that he'd been stunned when they examined the body after they found the bruised wrist?' She started sweating.

Detective Townsend replied, 'The doctor later noticed that the area where he was shot had been covered by something to disguise the puncture mark. His body changed colour once he was in the morgue and when they re-examined him, they found discolouration where the shot marks were.

'It looks as though the person who stunned Mr Reid came to the house with make-up to cover up the marks. After they analysed the paste, they concluded it was waterproof. This murder was planned, and the assailant was comfortable enough to put the make-up on and cover him back up again before he or she left the house.'

Erin was silent. She looked like a mannequin, staring into space. Rebecca asked, 'This person knew my dad and deliberately chose to hurt him?'

Mills answered, 'Yes they did, and they took nothing from the house. We also need to tell you the officers from the Forensic Unit will be coming over to try and get fingerprints.'

Rebecca raised her voice, 'It's a bit late for that,

everyone and their dog has been around already. All my friends, the neighbours, everyone. Are you saying it could be one of us? I think it's a fruitless exercise. Whoever did this to my dad is long gone. And do you suspect my mother or me? There were nail marks with the bruising on my dad's wrist. How do you know for sure it wasn't one of us?'

Detective Townsend answered, 'Miss Reid, now we know it's a murder investigation we have to leave no stone unturned. We are aware that the person who did this has a head start, but we still have to do our job and catch them.

'Regarding the bruising, we have ruled the two of you out because you have solid alibis, you were at work and had not left all morning. Mrs Reid said she had gone out shopping and we checked with the taxi company and the shops she said she visited that morning. The assistants from at least two of the shops have confirmed your mum was there. Her red hair made her easy to identify.'

Erin raised her eyebrows then spoke, 'So your checks are done already? Fast work.'

'We had to Mrs Reid, there is no time to waste,' said Detective Mills. 'Can you tell us why anyone might want to harm Mr Reid?' He looked at them.

Rebecca shifted in her chair uneasily, 'I don't know who would do that to him? Have you asked people at his workplace?'

He replied, 'We have, but they were all fond of him.

He had no arguments with anyone and the management liked him too.'

Erin then added, 'I can't think of anyone that wanted to harm him. I can understand someone wanting to hurt me. I'm sure I've ruffled a feather or two, but Finn! He was a lovely, kind man.'

'What about someone with a vendetta against the family?' asked Mills.

Rebecca responded, 'I can't think who would choose to do that to any of us. We are normal people with normal lives. This is way outside of the realms of things we worry about – we aren't a political family and we aren't celebrities that someone might want to harm. We live in a quiet street, with no problems with the neighbours or passers-by. I don't understand it.' She studied her mother sitting next to her at the dining table. She put out her hand to her mother who took it gratefully. They held hands whilst nobody spoke.

Then Rebecca said, 'Detective Mills, there is one thing I can think of, but I don't know if it's anything at all.'

Both the detectives stared at her with interest, Townsend spoke, 'Please tell us, Miss Reid, it might help.'

Cautiously, Rebecca looked at her mother then said, 'I know my dad wanted to tell me something. It was on his mind, but he couldn't come out and say it. It was as if he was hiding a secret.'

Erin interrupted, 'Don't be silly darling, what secret could he be hiding?'

Mills said with a steely voice, 'Please Mrs Reid, let her speak. Go on, Rebecca.'

'Hmmm… it might be nothing, but lately, my parents have been arguing. I thought it might have been my engagement to Matt, but I suspect it's more than that. I know he had something to tell me, and it was at the tip of his tongue, but he couldn't say it. Maybe it was something to do with why he was killed.'

The detectives looked at each other and then Mills asked, 'Thank you, Rebecca. Mrs Reid, can you shed a light on what caused the argument?'

Erin shifted uneasily in her chair. She pushed a lock of her hair behind her ear and said, 'It was nothing. Rebecca was right, it was mainly about her engagement to Matt Rook. I don't like him and Finn wanted me to change my mind for Rebecca's sake, so we argued about that.'

'So, are you aware of what your husband wanted to tell Rebecca? The secret that she thinks he was hiding?' asked Townsend.

'I think that's silly, Rebecca. He had nothing to hide. You know what your father is like!' She looked at her daughter, hoping she would agree with her.

'Dad was like an open book, but I felt there was something he wished to tell me. I was close to him, so I knew him well. And your arguments couldn't have been just because of my engagement. I think there was more to it.'

Erin snapped, 'Well there wasn't, and that's all I will

say on the matter!' she folded her arms in front of her and stared out the window.

Rebecca shrugged and looked at the detectives, then Erin spoke again, changing the topic, 'So, with the nail marks left on Finn, do you suspect the assailant to be a woman?'

'We won't rule anybody out Mrs Reid, it could be either. But a stun gun would be an easy way to over-power Mr Reid. With the nail impressions and bruising around his wrist and the make-up applied to his chest, it's easy to come to the conclusion that it was a woman. But we haven't ruled a man out yet.' Said Detective Townsend.

After asking more routine questions, the detectives left. Over the next twenty-four hours, the police exam-ined their house, photographing things, gathering finger-prints and looking for anything that was out of place. Erin admitted that she'd had a good look around, once she'd discovered how her husband had died, but had found nothing unusual. They questioned the neigh-bours, but they had seen nothing either. Everything was as it should have been, apart from Mr Finn Reid's strange death.

Frank, as usual, was a pillar of strength for Rebecca, but Matt was a hindrance. He was absent-minded, moody and sometimes silent for a long time.

Puja and Samuel were around a lot too, their jovial dispositions helped Rebecca forget the problems around her. Puja had now concluded it was only a matter of time before Rebecca broke her engagement off with

Matt and went out with Frank instead. Rebecca, of course, dismissed her out of hand, but deep within her, she knew Puja was right. But for now, she had too much to deal with, with her father's death. Her love life came last! Rebecca found herself constantly asking why she was wanting to remain engaged to Matt.' He seemed to prefer Molly's company and they hadn't had sex for two months. He instigated nothing when there were alone, and she was grateful for it. She felt like it had become a plutonic relationship.

Three weeks after her father's death, Rebecca decided she needed to go back to work. So, she asked Frank about returning after the funeral, now scheduled for a week's time. Although he welcomed her enthusiasm, he warned her it could be too soon.

Matt said she should take six months off, he didn't want her to be anywhere near Frank. Luckily for Rebecca, he never found out about Frank's visits to her house. Puja thought she needed to take more time to come to terms with her father's death and to allow two further weeks after the funeral.

Finn Reid's funeral went exactly as Rebecca had envisaged it. Erin and Rebecca didn't have to go to the funeral parlour. Frank arranged for the funeral directors to come over to their house to discuss all the plans. According to Finn Reid's wishes, he was cremated.

Matt wasn't happy that Frank was at the funeral, but Rebecca insisted she wanted him there, still not letting him know the finer details of Frank's involvement. It was none of his business, anyway. She was starting to get impatient with him. At one point at the wake, she looked at Molly and Matt laughing at a joke. She was not amused and scowled from afar. Frank, noticing her demeanour, came over to distract her.

Then later on, she noticed Molly trying to sink her claws into Frank – now that pissed her off no end! Her heart beat faster, her face flushed, and she wanted to storm over there and tell Molly to get out, but she knew she couldn't do that. Matt noticed her watching them and said, 'How are you holding up, Bec?'

Distracted by his question, she looked at him, smiled and replied, 'Hmm… ok, I guess.' Then she glanced back at Molly and Frank.

'Can't stop looking at him, hun?' His voice was like steel.

Rebecca frowned, she looked back at Matt, 'What? Are you talking about Frank?'

'Who else, Mr Perfect over there, talking to Molly. He can try all he wants, but he won't ever get her. She has class and style. He just tries for everyone's girl-friend. Molly knows his type!'

Rebecca felt her face glow hot, 'From here, it looks like Molly's doing all the flirting. Look at her leaning on him! This is a wake, not a nightclub!'

'Molly's not like that, she is decent and kind. He thinks he can get any girl. He can't have you, so he's latching onto Molly. Let me go and rescue her.' He too was becoming annoyed by Frank talking to Molly.

Without waiting for a response from Rebecca, he strode over and said something to them. Frank's face lost its smile, and he stormed off for the exit.

Rebecca didn't know what Matt had said to him or what to do. Erin came over to ask if she was ok. She said she was and watched her mother go off to check on other guests. Erin loved to play host, she was most comfortable in that role.

At last, Rebecca went home. She had an almighty headache, Matt drove her and her mum, with Molly tagging along. He said he would drop Molly off last and come back, but Rebecca said she was tired and drained and would be heading for bed as soon as she'd had a shower. Matt was content with that answer and drove away with Molly. Rebecca watched them leave and was glad they were gone for now.

The next morning, she went downstairs to speak to her mother. She decided to go back to work in a week's time. But when she entered the kitchen, she found her mother wasn't there. The front door was open, and there was no answer when Rebecca called out to her. Her heart started beating fast – had the person that killed her father now taken her mother? She ran out the front door, calling out to her mother hysterically. At the bottom of the drive, she saw a group of people near Mr and Mrs Crowe's house. She slowed her pace and saw her mother there, talking to one of the other neighbours and ran the last few paces to find out what was going on.

When Erin saw her, she said, 'Oh Rebecca, you're up. Something terrible has happened to Mr and Mrs Crowe, poor things. Their dog, little Lucy, died.'

Rebecca had been fond of Lucy. She was stunned and raked her hands through her hair to keep it from blowing in the wind. 'Oh no... they loved that little thing. I loved her too. What happened, did she run onto the road and get hit by a car? It always worried them she would do that.'

Erin whispered, 'Not exactly.'

'Well then?' Rebecca asked, why was her mum always so difficult to get answers out of?

Erin cleared her throat, 'They found her hanging from a rope tied to a tree at the end of their garden!'

Rebecca made an 'O' shape with her mouth and clapped her hands over it. How could someone be so cruel? She could think of nothing to say.

8

After comforting Mr and Mrs Crowe, Erin and Rebecca returned to their house. The Crowes' daughter had come to take over from the neighbours and look after her parents. Rebecca paced her living room floor, trying to make sense of why someone would do that to poor Lucy. She texted Puja, who was at work, she then rang Rebecca immediately after receiving the text. Puja asked if it was something to do with the neighbourhood. First her dad, now the dog, but Rebecca was sure they were unrelated.

When the detectives heard about the next-door neighbour's dog, they went straight over to interview the Crowes. Detective Chief Inspector Mills wanted to obtain the details from them whilst it was still fresh in their minds. They told him that they couldn't find Lucy in the morning, they searched for her everywhere, even the streets, in case she'd been run over by a car, but they didn't find her. Mr Crowe checked the garden but didn't see Lucy and then Mrs Crowe thought she might have gone to the far end. She had, on occasion, seen foxes at night, at the bottom of the garden and feared Lucy may have been attacked by them. When she looked there, she found Lucy, dangling from a tree and she screamed.

Mr Crowe had come running out when he heard her screaming, he wanted to rescue Lucy but her body was cold. She had been there for a few hours at least. The detective tried to ascertain whether they'd seen anything unusual the previous day or even today, but they said they hadn't. Everything had been normal. They couldn't understand who would deliberately set out to hurt Lucy. She was a friendly dog that didn't bark much unless there were strangers around. They also had a detached house, so no one would hear any noise Lucy made.

Detective Mills looked around the Crowes' house and garden, so he could figure out how someone could have lured Lucy out. He learned that the couple sometimes forgot to lock their back door – somebody may have come in and grabbed Lucy at night without them even realising it. But why do that to the old couple?

When Mr Crowe's daughter thought the detective had got all the information he required, she ushered him away, telling him her parents needed to grieve for Lucy in peace. Detective Mills walked over to the Reids' house to speak to Erin and Rebecca. He was aware that they had only buried Mr Finn Reid the day before, and things were still sensitive at home, so he was careful to say nothing that would upset them too much.

Erin welcomed him in, she was always glad to receive guests. She made him a cup of tea. Rebecca was there too, and he asked them more questions about the Crowes. The Reid's too had seen nothing, they couldn't think who would wish to harm Lucy. They confirmed that the Crowes had been to the funeral the day before and had been their usual selves.

The detective asked if the Reid's had heard of any other unusual deaths. Or if anyone else they knew had passed away recently. He wanted to see if there was a connection to the family.

What he found out stunned him. Rebecca told him that over the last four or five months, she had attended three funerals and missed a fourth her friend's, because she didn't find out she had died until after the funeral. She told the inspector about her paternal grandmother dying in her sleep, the suicide of Lara and Macy's stabbing and death – some of which Detective Mills already knew of.

The detective had a feeling that the deaths might be linked, but Rebecca said they seemed random and unfortunate. It was just a bad time or a bad year for the family. The detective didn't believe in coincidences, but he didn't want to upset them with his wild theories. Once he'd gathered more information – names and addresses of all the people that Rebecca had mentioned had died over the course of a few months – he took his leave and set about trying to investigate it further.

The first thing he did when he got to his car was call Detective Sargent Xavier Townsend. Townsend picked up on the third ring. 'Boss what is it? It's my day off.' He sounded like he was still in bed.

'For God's sake Xavier, it's nearly two in the afternoon, you lazy crud! Wake up – I need you in the office within the hour.' He spoke fast.

'Chris, do you know what it means when it's a day off? It means no work!'

'Xavier, can you take another day off instead? I promise you I will make sure you get a whole day back to make up for today.'

He knew if he was nice, Xavier wouldn't refuse him.

'Fine, fine, but I'm holding you to the day off. Now what's happened that's so urgent?'

'Get your ass into the office, and I will explain everything.'

With that, he rang off, he didn't need to involve anybody else for now. His theories might be wrong. He could trust Xavier to run with it until they had something concrete.

Over the next few days, Detective Mills and Townsend examined the doctor's death certificates for old Mrs Reid, Lara and Macy's deaths. They looked into the way Macy was killed, what times of the day they all passed away, and if there was any consistency to the deaths, but they came up blank every time.

Xavier said, 'Ok, so what we have so far is this – and correct me if I'm wrong: Old Mrs Reid passes away around five months ago in her bed. The two weeks before old Mrs Reid dies, Rebecca's friend Lara dies by committing suicide, also in her bed, by a lethal injection of heroin. The strange thing about the Lara suicide is that everyone said she was happy and didn't appear suicidal, but who knows what goes on behind closed doors! Oh, and nobody even knows if she ever took heroin regularly or whether it was just a one-off.

'Then a few days after she passes away, Mrs Macy Rook dies, stabbed by a robber who took her phone and handbag which was never recovered. The killer then dragged her under a bush where she bled to death, so nobody found her till a few hours later.

Then there was Mr Finn Reid, we have all the facts on him, and now the little dog, Lucy. Is that all we have on those deaths?'

Christopher nodded, 'Yes, all good so far and all unconnected to each other. What perplexes me is that there is no repetition to any of them. I don't know, Xavier, I could be over-thinking this!'

Xavier said, 'I know what you mean though, it all sounds like a big run of bad luck for the Reid family. I still have a niggling feeling that Mrs Reid is trying to hide something. She was very defensive about her arguments with her husband.'

'Yes, I was thinking about that and what they could have been arguing about, but if Erin Reid doesn't tell us, we may never know. It could be financial issues or general marital problems like something sexual, so maybe she was embarrassed. Well at least we attempted to piece everything together, but I don't think we can make it stick,' sighed Mills. 'We will still have to keep an open mind and watch that family closely. If anything happens, anyone else dies, we'll be the first on the scene.'

Xavier laughed, 'And that's why you're one of the best.'

Christopher laughed, 'I wouldn't say best, but I'm definitely like a dog with a bone.'

'I guess time will tell. If there is foul play, it won't go undiscovered for long.'

Christopher then said, 'Do you think Miss Rebecca Reid will talk to us if we ask to see her? I've got some questions I need to ask her about her friend, Lara.'

'I'm sure if we say we want to find out more about their friendship and do it with her mother or fiancé around, that way she won't have any objections.'

'Ok, I'll ring her and schedule a meeting for tomorrow. It's too early to do it today, they are too distraught, what with Mr and Mrs Crowe's dog dying and all.'

Rebecca got the call from Detective Mills later that day, to meet with him to discuss Lara. She wanted Frank to be with her when she spoke to the detectives, but he had to fly to Scotland for an emergency meeting, so she asked Matt to come with her as a last resort. She insisted that he didn't bring Molly. If she hadn't, Molly would have tagged along like a little puppy.

Rebecca didn't tell her mother anything, she met the detectives at the police station. After all, she had nothing to hide. She wasn't sure why they wanted to talk to her about Lara, but if they needed information about her friend, she was happy to oblige.

Matt and Rebecca arrived at the police station, and were promptly shown into an interview room. Once they were all settled, Detective Mills asked, 'Miss Reid, can you give me some background information about Lara Henderson?'

Detective Xavier sensed that Matt was feeling uneasy about being questioned in this way and said, 'Don't worry, nothing is being recorded and nobody even knows you are here. It's just some routine questions about her friend.'

Matt settled down, now they were all here sat together, they might as well get on with it. Rebecca was not tense at all. Matt watched her, *she looks like she does this all the time*.

Rebecca said, 'Please call me Rebecca. I've known Lara since primary school.'

She continued to tell them about their friendship, and told her story to the end, talking about her last meeting with Lara and how surprised she was when she found out that her friend had died. She stated that she had never known that Lara used heroin. Rebecca also described how one of the last things they'd done together had been to look at engagement rings. She hadn't appeared to be depressed or as if she was hooked on drugs.

The two detectives agreed that it was odd behaviour for her to appear one way then suddenly change. Mills said, 'Unless something drastic happened between when you met Lara and her death. But I am sure her parents would have known something. Did they suggest any such thing? Did Lara go through a mental breakdown before her death?'

'No, they were just as baffled, she appeared fine to them too.'

Next, they questioned her further about Matt's mother, Macy, and how friendly she had been with her. Matt got annoyed straightaway.

'Why do you need to know about my mother? I have been asked and answered all the questions you need. All you have to do is read the notes on the case.'

Detective Townsend answered, 'We have read the reports, Mr Rook, but we want to hear Rebecca's take on her relationship with your mother.'

Matt looked towards Rebecca, 'Bec, don't say anything you don't want to.'

She pleaded with him, 'Take it easy Matt, it's only a few harmless questions.' But she could see he wasn't pleased. She told them she had only met Macy Rook twice, and she hadn't known her that well.

Satisfied that that was all she could tell them, they said their goodbyes. The two detectives had made no progress and stopped looking into the other deaths. It was clear there were no connections between them.

Frank continued to visit Rebecca and Erin after nine or ten each evening. He apologised for not being with Rebecca when Mr and Mrs Crowe's dog died and for missing the interview with the detectives. She said it was no big deal. Frank, knowing she would start back at work soon, brought her up to speed on work issues. He noticed a change in her, she was more relaxed, and he knew, with the funeral over, she would be able to move forward.

Frank worried about Erin but didn't tell Rebecca. Erin was more withdrawn and seemed a lot less bubbly. He expected that, of course, but he suspected she was hiding something that was worrying her. Rebecca had mentioned the arguments her parents had been having, which always stopped suddenly when she was around. Maybe Finn had something he wanted to tell Rebecca without Erin finding out?

Frank never asked Rebecca about Matt – he didn't want to lose what he had built up with her. His uncle Logan wasn't impressed with him spending so much time with her. In his opinion, she was a taken woman and Frank would get his heart broken for a second time. But Frank didn't care. He still loved her and now she needed him more than ever, he would do his best to be there for her.

Rebecca was glad they were getting along so well, but she worried she was alienating Matt. She wondered if she was actually pushing Molly and Matt together.

She spent some time with Mr and Mrs Crowe that week, to keep them company and offer consolation. Considering what had happened, they were taking the tragedy well.

A few days later, she was feeling excited to be getting back to work. She was grateful to have something else to think about. Her work colleagues welcomed her back with a box of chocolates and a sympathy card. Frank bounced back to his business self and was professional in his communications with her. She had forgotten how handsome he looked in a suit. It made her heart beat quicker. She struggled to focus on clearing her mailbox from the stack of emails she had received whilst she'd been off. But it wasn't easy, and she could feel Frank's presence, even when he was in his own room and the door was closed.

She tried not to look at his office but was finding it hard to concentrate on work. Too much had happened since she'd last been here. She then reflected on the day Frank told her about her father's demise. He'd handled it well, he was the opposite of Matt. Cool, calm and collected, now she thought about it. What the hell was she doing with Matt?

Rebecca's first week at work went slower than she had expected. She had hoped the distractions of her private life would be pushed to the background, but this wasn't the case. Her mother, she noticed, had changed –

she was quieter than her usual, bubbly self. Matt was less interested in her – he didn't call, text or ask her over. Puja, as usual, texted and called her every day – this was a change. She knew Puja worried about her since the death of her father and was checking up on her more often.

Over breakfast, about two weeks after Rebecca had returned to work, Erin said, 'Darling, a letter came for you. I left it on the table over there. It looks strange. There's no stamp, so I guess it was hand delivered.'

She was surprised, 'No stamp? Wow, did you open it and check who it's from?'

'No, darling, it's your letter.'

Rebecca hurried into the kitchen and saw the envelope straight away. It was white, and on the outside, it said: '*To Rebecca, Private and Confidential*'. Someone had printed a white label and stuck it onto the envelope.

She flipped it over, there was nothing on the back. She opened it in a hurry. Her eyes widened and her heart began to race as she read the printed note that was inside.

"Dear Rebecca,

I feel it's my duty to tell you that you are being taken for a fool. Your fiancé Matt Rook is cheating on you with his ugly friend, Molly.

I have seen them frequently, frolicking around. Dump him, he doesn't deserve you. You're beautiful and can find someone 100 times better than him.

Trust me when I say, I have your best interests at heart.

Sending this, with all my love,

X"

Rebecca finished reading it, her legs felt weak, so she sat on the barstool and reread it. She wasn't sure if she was shocked about the implications that Matt was cheating on her, or the hand delivered letter itself.

9

Ten minutes later, Erin entered the kitchen to find Rebecca staring at the letter, 'Darling, what does it say?'

She handed it over to her mother.

Erin read it and looked at her sharply, 'Do you think this is true?'

Rebecca said in a quiet voice, 'I'm not sure Mum. I have to ask him. But who would send me a letter like this, see, it's typed up. As if the person wants to stay anonymous.'

Erin looked at the letter again, glancing at her daughter, she noticed she was on the verge of tears. She coaxed her, 'Rebecca you should discuss this with Matt, but you must tell Detectives Mills and Townsend about this letter. There could be someone that is targeting our family. First your dad, now you, who knows, I might be next on their list!'

'It's only a letter Mum, what if it's someone playing a prank? I'll feel a fool telling the police.'

'You won't. What if you say nothing and something happens? Would you like me to ring them?'

Rebecca pondered that suggestion for a moment, 'Ok, you call them and tell them I received the letter, and I will speak to Matt and find out what's going on. Did you hear anything, or see who might have posted it?'

'Not really, it was there, on the front door mat when I came down, but I'm sure it wasn't there last night because I double-check all the windows and doors at night. After what's happened, I'm not taking any chances. We also have the strange case of Mr and Mrs Crowe's dog. Because they left their back door open by mistake, look what happened to little Lucy.'

Rebecca zoned out for a few moments then exclaimed, 'So, someone posted it at night! We have to tell the detectives, this is disturbing.'

'Yeah, and it's scary. The detectives need to sort this out. We shouldn't have to live in fear.' Erin said, shivering.

She hadn't seen this side of her mother, and she didn't want to worry her.

'We will speak to the detective, Mum, don't worry. You call them as planned, let me take a picture of the letter, that way, if they take it away, I can still show Matt what it said.'

Erin looked pleased her daughter had agreed to get the detectives involved.

After taking the picture, she called Matt, he didn't answer. It annoyed her, so to prove a point she rang Molly, who picked up her phone within two rings.

Rebecca tried to sound calm, 'Morning Molly, sorry to bother you so early on a Saturday morning, but I need to ask if you've seen Matt?'

Molly giggled, 'Morning Beckie, of course I have. I'm at his house now. We went out last night, and he let me stay over.'

Rebecca took a sharp intake of breath, she was speechless. A million things ran through her head. Was the letter right after all? And if it was, could that person be spying on them? Why did they want to help her, and could they want something in return? And why was Molly so nasty to her? She knew they hadn't crossed paths before, so why did Molly take pleasure in taunting her?

'Beckie, are you still there?' Molly asked dragging her back to reality.

'Yes, yes, I'm here.' But suddenly, she could wait no longer, she needed to know now, so she asked, 'Molly, is there something going on between the two of you?'

Molly laughed. 'Something like what, Beckie?'

Rebecca exploded, 'I told you not to call me Beckie! Now, are you two sleeping with each other or not?' Her heart was racing, and she could feel her face reddening.

'Beckie darling, when you shout that way, I can't speak to you. Learn to control yourself girl. Goodbye!'

'Molly, don't you dare put the phone down on me!'

Rebecca screamed, but it was too late, the line went dead.

Erin overheard everything, she frowned, and her eyes narrowed, then she came over to placate her. 'That woman is a bitch, darling. You wait till I get my hands on that dirty waste of space who calls himself your fiancé! I'll wring his bleeding neck!'

'Mum please, we don't know they are sleeping together for sure. I need to ask him.'

'What did that vile woman say?'

'Nothing much, just that she stayed over last night. She didn't say whether they slept together, she just implied it.'

It incensed Erin, 'I bet they have, I don't trust either of them, and you shouldn't listen to her. Go over there and confront them. I'm coming too. Let me get changed.'

'Mum, no, I will handle it. What if that message was meant to cause trouble?'

'But she stayed the night at his house? That's unacceptable, you should break off with that lowlife. Ever since his mum passed away, he's been a different person. He wasn't even there for you when Dad died, all he's done is frolic with that revolting hussy. That letter was right about one thing, she is ugly!

'Frank, now that's what you call a man. He's stayed by our side through everything. You must see how lucky you are to have him dote on you. We both are, darling. It's nice having a man around, you can't call that bloody

Matt a man! You're better off without him, I hope you can see that.' She finished with aplomb.

Rebecca let her mum rant on, she was listening, but she stared into space as well. She was thinking that whatever happened, she needed to break off with him. Whether or not he'd slept with Molly. He was spending more time with Molly than she was with Frank. Thinking about Frank again made her remember how much she was attracted to him. God, what was wrong with her?

Erin said, 'You ok, darling? Shall I get dressed?' Her voice was gentle.

Rebecca snapped out of her trance and said, 'No, Mum. Let me go there and talk to him myself. I can't have you fight my battles.'

She smiled at her mother, she wanted to prove to her she could handle it herself. 'Mum, whilst I am gone, call the detectives. Keep the letter with you, I've got a copy on my phone. And don't handle it too much. The detectives may want fingerprints from it.'

Erin nodded, 'Ok darling. You go and get ready.'

Ten minutes later, Rebecca said she was leaving for Matt's house. As she drove, she puzzled over it – what if Frank had sent the letter to try and end her engagement to Matt? She immediately dismissed it, it wasn't something Frank would do. It was so childish to send a letter like that, Frank would confront them rather than go out in the middle of the night to deliver a typed up letter. Plus, Frank was getting to spend time with her, he could make a move on her, he was in a better position now than in a long time. He wouldn't jeopardise that.

She got there quicker than she expected, there was little traffic and her mind had been full of thoughts of Matt and Molly. She imagined them sleeping together, and it surprised her that she had no feelings of jealousy about it. Molly was needy and Matt was acting like a fool – in her opinion, they deserved each other and she would be well out of it. She wanted to find out what Matt's defence would be when she told him about her conversation with Molly this morning.

When she got there, Matt opened the door very quickly. He must have been expecting her. He gave her a broad smile, 'Hey Bec, come in, now wait to hear what I have to say before you go *"all guns blazing"* on me, I can explain.'

Rebecca didn't even have time to say anything, 'This will be interesting,' she thought. She gave him a stare, and she stormed past him. She looked around for Molly, she turned to face him. 'So where is your *good friend*, Molly?'

'Bec, darling, don't be like that. Don't worry, she isn't here. I sent her home.' He came over to her, he tried to put his hands on her shoulders to calm her. She shrugged them off.

'Please don't touch me, Matt – I can't bear it after what you've been getting up to with her!' she spat.

'Bec, I promise you, I didn't sleep with her last night, or ever. We have never even kissed. I love you, you're my girl. Why would I do that to you?'

She was wondering when she should show him the letter. But she said nothing for now. 'So, you didn't sleep with her, but you let her stay the night?'

'I see nothing wrong with being close friends with Molly. You have been so preoccupied, so I thought I'd let you deal with your family issues in peace.'

'Let me "*deal with my family issues*"!' she repeated. 'When I need you the most, you prefer that I deal with it all on my own? I was here with you every step of the way when your mother died, I rather expected the same. Obviously that was too much to ask.' She tried to keep her voice calm. Her nerves were all over the place.

'I didn't want you here when my mum died, you were a hindrance!' Anger rose in him too. 'I was giving you space, something you never gave me!' he retorted.

'If you needed space, why on earth didn't you say so? And if you wanted to do things with anyone, why Molly? I know that she hates me and is somehow jealous of me. I have told you this, but you don't seem to care.'

Matt put up his hands and shouted, 'Enough Rebecca!' She stopped in her tracks. 'I have explained everything, if you don't want to listen and want to be a crybaby, then do it somewhere else!'

She gasped, she couldn't believe he felt entitled to be annoyed. She calmed herself, 'Matt, can I ask you one question, and please answer truthfully. Why do you want to marry me?'

He wasn't expecting that question and didn't speak for a few seconds as he thought about the answer.

He then said, 'Firstly because I love you and I know things changed between us after my mother died. I hoped that by us solidifying our commitment, we could get back to when we were happiest.'

That was all the motivation Rebecca needed to break off her engagement, there is no point in marrying someone in the hope it will fix a relationship. It should be solid at the point of marriage.

So, she decided now was the time to tell him about the letter and then about breaking their engagement. Plucking up courage, she got her phone out, 'You'd better take a look at this.'

She showed him the photo of the letter she received from the unknown recipient. He said, 'What is this?'

'Read it. It's about you and Molly, other people are noticing the pair of you frolicking, it isn't just me!'

He read it twice. He handed the phone back to her. 'Where did you get this?'

'Someone posted it through my letter box by hand last night, there wasn't a stamp on it. It was addressed it to me.'

He reflected on it for a moment, she could see his confusion but his anger had subsided. He said, 'Well I'm telling you, nothing is going on between us, no matter what that letter says.'

'Then why did that person say that? They must know something.'

'I don't give a fuck what they know. They're an asshole, Molly isn't ugly!'

'You're angry because they called Molly ugly?' She

couldn't believe he'd just said that. 'How can you stand there still defending her? The person who wrote the letter got it right, you were in the same house last night. For all I know, maybe in the same bed too!'

'Well we weren't, and I suspect Frank sent that to you to split us up.'

It was her turn to be on the defensive, 'Frank wouldn't be that petty, he is a grown man, not a child. If he had a problem with you and Molly, then he would have told me to my face, not in a letter.'

'Oh now you want to protect your precious Frank!'

Rebecca didn't want to start a fresh argument with him which now included Frank, she was drained by Matt so she said, 'You know what? I'm not sure there is a point to this engagement anymore Matt. I loved you at one stage, but a marriage isn't a sticking plaster for a relationship gone wrong,' she removed the ring he'd given her, 'it's a commitment between two people who love each other,' and she handed it back.

He took it. 'Maybe you're right. Someone better than you deserves this ring. Someone who hasn't got her nose in the air looking down on everyone from her high and mighty throne!'

She shook her head, this was getting petty and horrible. Without another word, she walked out of his house. She wasn't even angry anymore. She was sad that they had to end it, she had wanted them to part amicably, not like this.

10

R ebecca wanted to ring Frank and cry on his shoulder, but she wasn't sure if she should burden him with her problems. She drove around in circles for a while, not wanting to go home to face her mother, and then directed her car towards Frank's apartment.

It was not even eleven in the morning – she hoped Frank was at home. When she got there, she rang his doorbell a few times. He didn't answer. She could swear she'd seen his car in his usual parking bay. Just as she was about to leave, the door opened. Frank looked surprised to see her standing there. And she was surprised too, not because the door had opened at last, but because all Frank had on was a white towel tied around his waist and another draped around his neck. His hair was still wet from his shower, his chest was bare.

He noticed her expression, 'Hi Frey, sorry, I was in

the shower. I would have dressed up if I'd known you were coming, I thought it was the mailman with a parcel. I told him I'd prefer to have it delivered to my door if possible – I always give him a fiver for his troubles, so he's extra nice. I do hope you aren't put off by my state of undress,' he grinned.

'Oh, my God,' she thought, what was he doing to her? He had even more defined abs than she remembered, she figured he must be spending more time in the gym these days. She hadn't imagined his body was like that. But now she could see it nearly bare, she was shocked – and turned on. She forced herself to snap out of it.

'Frank, sorry, I didn't mean to stare.' She might as well be honest with him. 'I don't remember you looking this…' her voice trailed off.

'Fit, sexy, hot, god dammed gorgeous?' he laughed. 'Trust me, I will take any of them!' *His face lights up when he smiles.*

'…Hmmm, I guess.'

'But where are my manners, please come in, we can't carry on talking here. It'll give my neighbours something to gossip about.' He stood aside to let her in.

As he shut the door he asked, 'So what brings you here on a fine Saturday morning?'

Rebecca was so distracted by Frank's practically naked body that she had almost forgotten the reason for her visit.

'Why don't you put some clothes on first, I feel overdressed, I don't really want a serious conversation with you in a towel!' she said trying to look directly at his eyes so that they didn't stray over to his body again!

'We can fix that, I can always bring you towels, then we'll be on level ground.' He laughed at the shocked look that flashed across her face. 'Ok, loosen up, I was just kidding. Give me two minutes. Make yourself comfortable,' he was still grinning as he spun around and headed towards his bedroom.

She drew a deep breath, without knowing it, she'd been holding it. Only an hour ago, she'd broken her engagement to Matt, and here she was, getting seriously turned on by Frank! She stilled her breathing and counted slowly from twenty down to one.

He was back before she'd finished her countdown. He had combed his hair neatly. He wore grey tracksuit bottoms, and a plain white cotton top now covered his chest. Frank was always effortlessly on trend, and as usual, his feet were bare.

'I'm making coffee Frey, would you like one? Or tea, your usual?' he asked.

'Yes please, I'll have a coffee.'

'Ok, hang on a minute, I'll be back soon.' He turned towards the kitchen to make it.

'I'll come with you.'

He yelled over his shoulder, 'I went for a run this morning, so I'm starving, I'm making toast too. Do you want some? Or eggs and bacon?'

She remembered she hadn't eaten anything yet, she should have been hungry, but she wasn't. After receiving the strange letter, then breaking off her engagement with Matt and the thrill of seeing Frank's nearly naked body, food was the last thing on her mind.

'I'm ok thanks, you go ahead though.'

'Ok cool, so what's got our Frey all het up this morning? Well, apart from my near nakedness!' He laughed, and she frowned.

Rebecca wanted to laugh, and she felt uncomfortable trying to stifle it, 'I think you might be a bit in love with yourself.'

He continued busying himself in the kitchen, 'Well someone has to be,' he smiled. 'And don't make that face, I can see you're trying not to laugh. Just give in to it, laugh if it's funny!' He was enjoying taunting her.

At last, she cracked a smile, 'Ok, that was funny, I'll give you that!'

'So?' he asked.

Realising she hadn't answered his question, she said, 'It's been a heck of a day! I needed to talk to someone sensible.'

'Well, go on, spill.'

'When I got up this morning, my mum told me a hand-delivered letter had arrived for me.'

His toast popped, 'Interesting, another admirer?' he asked, smiling.

'Ok, Frank, eat your damn toast, and afterwards, we can talk in peace. You're too distracted and you're not taking me seriously.'

'Now that's a good idea. I can't do anything properly when I'm hungry.'

She watched him whilst he was eating his toast. He

was the opposite of Matt, what the hell had she been playing at getting engaged to that idiot. Thank the lord she'd called off the engagement. Now, sat here, she struggled to think why she hadn't pursued a relationship with Frank instead.

'Ok, done,' he said, wiping the back of his hand and across his mouth, bringing Rebecca back to reality.

'So, I told you I got this letter, right?'

'Ah, huh.' he nodded.

'Well, it was typed, and even the envelope addressed to me had a printed label on the front.'

'Printed? What do you mean, it was an official letter? From an office?'

'No, I mean printed from a printer, here, look at it. I took a photo.' She fished out her phone and showed him the letter.

His face clouded over, and he changed in an instant. One minute he was jovial but now he was dead serious, 'Frey, this is strange. Have you called the police?'

'What, about the content?' she asked.

'This isn't good, first, someone killed your dad, then the next-door neighbour's dog gets strangled in the middle of the night, and now this letter! When did it arrive?'

'Last night.' Her voice quietened down, he was right. Never mind the content, this was very strange. Now she had been alarmed by it and was going to contact the police.

'If you haven't told the detectives yet, we should do it immediately.' He looked troubled.

'My mum will call them. I told her not to handle the letter too much, they might want to test it for fingerprints.'

'Yes, good idea, so you came straight here after you found it?'

She hesitated, 'Well no, I called Matt to see if what the letter claimed was true, but he didn't answer, so I called Molly…' she trailed off.

'And?'

'Hmm… she told me she'd spent the night at Matt's house.'

'Are they crazy? Is Matt mad or blind? He's got you, and he runs around with her?'

'She didn't say they'd got up to anything, but then she put the phone down on me, so I drove over there, I needed to find out from him. I don't trust anything she says.

'Oh, and what did they say?' He studied her intently, his eyes narrowed.

'She'd gone, so I spoke to Matt alone.' She related their heated exchange. His expression changed several times and when she was done, she could see he was enraged.

'Well you did the right thing, and you can ignore his suggestion that it was me who delivered the letter. If I'd seen them together, I'd have told you to your face! You know you're better off without him. He is so immature, Frey, surely you deserve much more than that?'

'The thing is, I'm not angry with him. To be blunt

Frank, I don't give a shit if they slept together! I want nothing more to do with him.'

'Good for you, now let's not dwell on that. Let me come with you, we need to go back to your place to speak to your mum, I want to find out what the detective makes of this.'

Rebecca nodded, and they finished their coffee quickly. When they got to Rebecca's house, her mum hugged her immediately, 'Oh God, there you are, I was worried. You've been gone ages!' Then, noticing Frank, she added, 'Hello Frank, I didn't see you standing there. Did Rebecca tell you about the letter?'

'Hi Erin, yes she did. Did you ring the detective?'

She nodded, 'They should be here shortly.'

Rebecca asked, 'Why were you worried, Mum? Has something else happened?' She searched her mother's face intently for an answer.

'No, nothing more than the letter. I was worried about what Matt was saying to you and whether that vile girl was there too. I didn't want them to gang up on you. So, what did Matt say? Did he admit they were sleeping together?'

She looked relieved, the last thing she wanted to hear was that another unfortunate incident had occurred whilst she'd been out. 'Not really, when I got there, only Matt was home.' As Rebecca finished telling her mother the story, Erin looked happily at them, 'At bloody last, I couldn't wait for you to get rid of that useless waste of space!' she laughed.

Rebecca frowned, 'Mum, for God's sake.' She stole a look at Frank, but he was smiling too.

He asked, 'So where is this typed letter?'

Frank and Rebecca looked in the direction of the kitchen counter where Erin was gesturing.

'Rebecca can you open it, please? Let me read it. I don't want to get my fingerprints on it. The police might assume it was me who sent it if my prints are on it, and that wouldn't be good.'

Rebecca picked up the letter and opened it to show him what was written inside. He frowned, reading it, shaking his head. 'Hmmm, it's strange, very strange indeed.'

Just then, there was a knock on the back door. They had informed Erin that the detectives would enter the house from the kitchen door because they wanted to dust the front door for prints. Erin and Rebecca greeted Detectives Mills and Townsend and introduced them to Frank.

Rebecca handed them the letter, which they took after putting on gloves. They, too, agreed that this was a strange way of giving her advice. They asked Rebecca if she knew of anyone who could possibly gain from their breakup or wish to put a strain on their relationship.

Rebecca and Frank glanced at each other, then she said, 'Well, Frank and I were close in the past, but we're just good friends now.'

Detective Mills whistled and stared at Frank. 'Did you type this up and post this in Rebecca's postbox?'

He looked shocked, 'Why would I do that? If I'd

wanted to warn her, I'd have done it in person. I don't work in such an underhand manner, you can ask anyone.'

Detective Mills nodded, 'Don't worry Mr Pearson, pardon me for being blunt, but we will check it out. We rarely take people's word.'

Frank shrugged, then Mills said, 'Ok the forensic investigators will be here to dust for prints. They will also examine footsteps around your front garden and the front door. Please bear with us. To be honest with you, I don't think we will find any fingerprints. Footsteps, however, there may be, and, they can cross-reference our new footstep database to determine if it matches any we have on file.

'Whoever sent that letter would have needed to have been careful, as they posted it in the box. Apart from Frank, "*your special friend*", Rebecca, can you think of anyone who else might say such a thing and why?'

Frank spoke before Rebecca had a chance, 'Hey, I'm standing right here detective, you don't have to be rude!'

Mills replied, 'Just stating the facts, but what are you doing here?'

Rebecca spoke before an argument could escalate, 'Actually detective, I invited him. So, about your question, Molly could have sent it, trying to be clever. Implicating herself so we wouldn't suspect her of sending it and then achieve her aim of breaking my engagement with Matt.'

Detective Townsend, who had been quiet until now

added, 'That's a good point. Your mum told us you confronted Matt this morning. Did you find out anything?'

For the third time, Rebecca told her story of what had happened at Matt's house. She was getting fed up of re-hashing the whole thing again and again, but she did it patiently.

When she was finished, Detective Mills said, 'So, whoever it was appears to have got what they wanted?'

Rebecca shrugged. 'I guess so. But I believe they did me a favour. I was frustrated with Matt and Molly spending time together, and their total lack of sensitivity about my dad.'

Detective Townsend asked, 'Do you think the person that send your letter may have had your best interests at heart then?'

Detective Mills chipped in, 'That could be a reason, but not if we're assuming it was the same person who killed Mr Reid. They would have known that would cause upset to the family. Maybe we are looking at two different people. We will try to put the pieces together. In the meantime, be vigilant, don't go anywhere alone.' Turning to face Erin, he said, 'You too, Mrs Reid.'

Erin and Rebecca glanced nervously at each other. Up to now, they hadn't been too concerned for their own safety, but with this new warning from the police, they became very alarmed.

Frank reassured them, 'Don't worry. I'll be here to make sure they stay safe. When Mr Reid passed away, I came around every evening from nine or ten p.m. and left at about midnight. Erin is diligent in checking the house is safe, including making sure they lock their windows and doors.'

Detective Mills said, 'Good work Mrs Reid, stay vigilant. Now let me call the Forensics Unit.'

The morning turned to afternoon and then evening. The Forensics Unit took the prints they needed. They also found footprints outside, it was from a pair of boots that didn't belong to either of the Reid ladies. They were of someone with a shoe size six or seven. Erin and Rebecca both confirmed they hadn't been near the flower beds recently. It looked like the person that delivered the letter had peered through their windows at some point the night before.

Rebecca, Erin and Frank had dinner out that evening. Frank insisted they get out of the house, and away from their problems. The night went well, and Frank kept them entertained with jokes and funny stories. Rebecca got the feeling that Erin was flirting with him, she noticed her mother fiddling with her hair and giggling at everything Frank said. But she knew what her mother was like, she always had to take centre stage.

When they got back home, Erin looked tired, but she still offered to make Frank a coffee. He told her he could help himself – after spending so much time there, he knew where everything was – but she insisted. She said she would pop the kettle on and be back to make him a coffee.

Frank went around the house with Rebecca,

checking to see if anything looked out of place. He wanted to ensure no one was coming in and out of the house whilst they were out. After they were both were satisfied that no one had been in, they went down to the kitchen. Rebecca made him his coffee and herself tea as her mother wasn't back down yet.

Whilst they were sipping their drinks, they heard Erin, 'Oh, Frank, I told you I would make your coffee. I wanted to get out of my day clothes and into something more comfortable.'

They both looked at Erin, Rebecca couldn't believe her mother. She had changed into a black silk, knee-length dressing gown with a lace trim on the hem, neck-line and sleeve edges. 'Mum! Why are you wearing that?'

Erin's eyes were alight, 'I bet you won't look this good in twenty-five years' time!' she said then laughed as if she was joking.

This type of behaviour was not new to Rebecca, but to try to seduce Frank like this was wrong and very embarrassing. She would have to have a talk with her when they were alone. Rebecca recalled her mother had done this before with new boyfriends. As if she wanted them to choose her over her daughter. She had always behaved this way, and Rebecca had tried to discuss it with her in the past, but she never changed her ways. It was as if those conversations had never happened.

Erin glared at Rebecca, then smiled at Frank and said she was going to bed.

After she'd gone, Frank asked, 'Frey, can I be straightforward with you?'

She wasn't sure what he was going to say, 'You can always be honest with me. Are you annoyed that my mum came down half-dressed to seduce you? Trust me, she behaves inappropriately sometimes. I have tried, but she doesn't listen.' She smiled in an attempt to make light of her mother's behaviour.

Frank looked at her seriously and her smile quickly faded, 'Oh, what? Why are you looking at me that way?'

He sighed then said, 'I'm not happy the two of you are here alone, Frey. Now knowing what we know, the same person that killed your father could have stabbed Matt's mother. I know the police have looked into both cases to see if there's a link, and there appears to be none but…' he trailed off.

'But what?' she asked.

'But I'm not convinced whether it's a run of bad luck or something sinister. And I'm inclining towards the sinister!' His eyebrows knitted together, and he looked at her, waiting for a response.

Rebecca turned away from him, she circled around the kitchen, thinking about Frank's suggestions. He let her be and after a minute, she turned to him and said, 'I'm worried too, and I guess my mum is as well. She hasn't been her normal self since the detectives suggested foul play, and tonight she was something else. It's almost as if she knows what's going on but is afraid to say anything.' She sighed. 'Either way, apart from being vigilant, I don't know what more we can do.'

Frank felt sorry for her, he could see this was taking its toll on her. 'Why don't you both stay with me? I've got a guest bedroom and you could share with Erin for a while. What do you think, Frey?'

She responded instantly, 'Are you kidding? How long can we stay there with you? As far as we know, the detectives may never find who killed my father. As yet, they have found nothing apart from what killed him!'

Frank raked his hands through his hair, 'Yeah you're right.' He walked over to her, and without saying, he grabbed her shoulders and gave her a hug. She yielded to his embrace, and they stayed like that for a minute, Frank stroked her hair as if he was soothing a child. He took in deep breaths of her fragrant hair.

Rebecca felt content, relaxed and happy. She pulled away just enough to look into his eyes, tiptoeing slightly, she kissed him on his lips, surprising them both. She remained there, unable to move, and he bent closer to kiss her back, their kiss deepening in intensity.

Frank knew this had been a long time coming. But he had needed for her to want him. The kiss quenched his thirst for her. She was so soft, warm, inviting, and he wanted more. But then reality hit him. He couldn't take advantage of her, it wouldn't be fair. She wanted him, but what if this was a rebound reaction?

Rebecca moaned with pleasure, it took all his strength to stop. He knew they both didn't want that right now, but he had to make sure she was doing this for the right reasons. He pulled away from her, she opened her eyes, 'Frank?'

'We need to take it slow, Frey, I don't want you to do something you'll regret tomorrow.'

'S…sorry, Frank… I just…' she looked deflated, her breathing was returning to normal.

He smiled, looking at her, 'My God Frey, there is nothing I want more than to make love to you right here and now! But we can't, we need to be sure, I need to be sure you're not doing this…'

'As a rebound?' She could tell he wanted her as much as she wanted him. But what if he was right? What if she hurt him again? She couldn't do that to him. He was right, they needed to wait.

Frank replied, 'And with your recent loss, you may not be thinking straight.'

'Maybe you're right, let's take this one step at a time. We shouldn't rush into anything.'

His heart sank, they were both in agreement, but he wanted her right now too. He had half hoped she wouldn't agree with him!

Just then, they heard a sound outside. It was faint and sounded like a sneeze. They looked at each other for a few seconds, Rebecca said, 'Was that a sneeze?'

Frank was quick off the mark – he ran to the back door, unlocked it to see whoever was outside. As his eyes adjusted, he saw a woman driving a black Clio speeding away, but he couldn't make out who it was. They had parked the car a little way down the road to provide a swift getaway and avoid being seen.

Frank rushed into the road to see if he could glimpse the number plate, but it all happened too fast. He walked back to Rebecca, getting his breathing back. When he got within earshot he said, 'Know anyone who drives a black Renault Clio? She raced off too quickly for me to get her number.'

Rebecca was shivering, and her heart was still beating fast. 'A woman? With a Clio?' She tried to think quickly, but her brain was too fuzzy from kissing Frank then chasing a possible intruder or killer or whoever she was. After locking the kitchen door behind them, he directed her to the breakfast bar stool to sit and then he closed the blinds. 'This is ridiculous,' he thought, now they have to shut their curtains and blinds too?

He said firmly to Rebecca, 'Look – I think you should go to bed and try to sleep this off. I'll come up, just to make sure you're safe, and will then sleep on the couch in the living room. You two can't be on your own tonight. Thank God your mum is none the wiser!'

Rebecca nodded her head in acceptance. She was too drained to speak.

11

The door to Crofts and Castles burst open. 'I want to see Frank Pearson right now!' Matt wasn't happy.

Hearing the commotion, Frank stepped out of his room. He recognised the back of Matt Rook, and he could tell this meant trouble. He glanced over at Rebecca's desk, but it was empty. He could see the receptionist, Pamela, was having difficulty calming him down. The other staff members also stood up from their desks, partly to help Pamela but also to find out what was going on. The only sound in the room was from Matt yelling.

Frank strode over at speed, 'Matt, hi, if you're here for me, then would you like to step into my office?'

'Where is my Bec?' he continued to shout.

'His Bec?' thought Frank. With resolve he said, 'Matt please, stop upsetting my staff, come let's talk in my room.' He took Matt's elbow and gestured to his office.

Matt yelled, 'Don't fucking touch me, you scumbag! I know what a snake you are, and I'm here to make sure I take my Bec away from you!'

Frank felt the blood rush to his face, he was glaring at Matt now, too. How dare he come here and call him a snake and demand for Rebecca? They weren't even a couple anymore. He tried to calm himself or his staff would see him punch Matt, which would not be a pretty sight.

'What the hell is going on here? Matt is that you?' Rebecca had returned from her coffee break to find the office in chaos. Everyone was standing facing the reception area, so at first, she could only hear Matt.

They all stared at Rebecca. Matt said, 'Yeah, Bec, it's me, I've come to get you. Molly told me how this bastard tried to kiss and molest you.'

Rebecca put her hands on her now reddening cheeks and glared at him, everybody now turned their gaze to Frank.

Frank, saw her embarrassment, 'Matt, not only are you making a mistake, you're making a fool of yourself too. Please stop these wild accusations. If you can't behave, I will call the police to remove you from this office.'

'Come on Bec, let's go,' begged Matt.

Rebecca was flustered why is he here creating a scene, they weren't even together anymore. How did he find out Frank and her had kissed? At last, she found her voice and said, 'Matt, I ended our engagement a few days ago – something to do with a girl you had over for the night, if I remember correctly. Are you drunk, or have you lost your memory?'

Frank smirked, and Matt saw him, he stormed over to her, but Frank held him back. 'You dirty bitch! Molly caught the two of you kissing in your house last night. God knows what else might have happened too. I'm here to tell *him* to keep his filthy hands off you and to take you back home with me. I'll forgive and forget the kiss and whatever else you got up to. Let's go now!' He fought wildly against Frank's hold, 'Fucking get off me!'

Rebecca's blush deepened to the same colour as her hair, 'What gives you the right to come here and order me around? You have a one-track mind. You know what? We're over! And that is because of Molly, you're free to have her, and she you. You two deserve each other. What kind of person comes to my house at night to snoop on me? I will report her to the detectives, for all we know, with these night-time excursions of hers, she was the one who strangled poor Mr and Mrs Crowe's dog. Go on, get out of here!'

Matt glowered at her, he was breathing hard, but Frank was still holding on to him, so he stood rooted to the spot. After a few seconds, he said, 'And don't think I don't know about Frank's late-night visits to your house. And you let him pay for your father's funeral? Thank God for Molly, she gleaned that nugget of information from Sam at the funeral. I'm also aware about how he's been trying to push me out. I innocently believed everything you said! I bet you two have been carrying on behind my back for years. No wonder you don't want to leave this office! I should have known. Frank—'

Frank grabbed him by the back of his coat collar, 'Enough.' Dragging Matt towards the exit, 'you have outstayed your welcome, little man!'

Matt tried to turn around and punch Frank, but he was too strong and Frank used brute force to get him out. 'Get off me,' roared Matt. 'I won't forget this!'. Rebecca, you're a worthless bitch because of your looks…'

They heard nothing more as the door closed behind them, and one by one they walked towards Rebecca to check if she was ok. She stood frozen, still watching the door.

She was worried about Frank. Giving a brief smile to her colleagues coming towards her, she said, 'Let me check on Frank.'

Lisa was fond of both Frank and Rebecca, 'Please don't Rebecca, it might make Matt worse. He's already out of control!'

Just then, Logan, who had been making a phone call in another office, emerged to find out what the commotion was all about. He was only down for two days to check up on the London office. Lisa filled him in on what had happened and Logan sprang into action, 'I'll go, he won't be able to mess with both of us!'

'Ok fine, hurry, please,' begged Rebecca.

Logan ran outside. Lisa told Rebecca to sit down, she was shaking like a leaf.

Outside, Frank flung Matt onto the grass. Matt jumped up and shouted, 'You will never get my Bec, she only left me because you won't leave her alone! You had your chance with her and couldn't keep her, so what makes you think you will this time?'

Frank's voice was quiet but stern, 'Shut the hell up, you're the one who can't keep her. She wants to be with me now, and who knows, we might even get married!

'She will string you along as she did me, just you watch!'

Frank had had enough and turned away to leave. Suddenly Logan shouted, 'Watch out Frank, he's charging for you!'

Frank looked around just in time, Matt lunged at him, but Frank stuck his elbow out to block Matt, who cried out in pain, Frank's elbow had connected with Matt's chest. 'You hurt me, I will report you to the police,' he bawled.

Frank could handle himself but was pleased to hear Logan say, 'You can if you want mate, but I'm a witness, and I saw you trying to attack Frank – he was defending himself. He should have punched you, but he is too good. If it was me, I would have happily done it for sure. So, why don't you do us all a favour and piss off? I'm warning you now, I'm not as sophisticated as my handsome nephew here. I've got friends that aren't very nice, so don't get me annoyed enough to ring them. Although, it would give me no better pleasure. From what I gathered in there, you're nothing but hot stale air! Now, go on, fuck off!'

Both men watched Logan in amazement, Matt because for the first time today, he felt afraid and Frank because he had never seen that side of his uncle before – and was impressed! Frank and Logan looked at each other, then at Matt, who was still rubbing his chest. But he had nothing more to say, he turned away and stormed off.

Frank clapped his uncle's back and smiled, 'Didn't know you had it in you, uncle, that was a class speech! Even I was scared of you at one point.'

Both men laughed, 'I rarely show my darker side.' He winked at Frank.

The staff were still unsettled when they got in, so Frank told his uncle he'd like to address everyone immediately. 'Everybody, gather around please.' He scanned the room, looking for a Rebecca and saw her talking to Lisa, it looked like Lisa was trying to calm her.

There were seven of them – it wasn't a large office. Two of his staff were out at meetings. Once he had their attention, he said, 'I would like to apologise for today's incident. If anyone felt threatened or uncomfortable and wish to speak to me privately about it, I will make time for them. Some of you may be familiar with Matt Rook, the man who came in just now. He is Rebecca's ex-fiancé, Rebecca, I hope you don't mind me telling everyone.'

Rebecca nodded her head, so he continued,

'Rebecca recently broke off her engagement to him after she had a tip-off that another girl – Molly, was not only spending time with him but was staying overnight too. Rebecca felt she didn't want to continue the engagement and ended it.

Last night, when I was at Rebecca's house, we heard something outside and ran out to have a look. We saw a woman drive off in a haste, and we now know it was Molly spying on Rebecca. Obviously, Molly isn't of sound mind or she wouldn't snoop around like that.

I'm still not clear why he barged in here to demand that Rebecca go with him, since they are no longer engaged. In future, if he turns up, can one of you call the police at once, and if Rebecca is in the office, make sure she goes to the back, so he can't talk to her. Now, have any of you got questions?'

Nobody spoke, so he said, 'Excellent, thanks, you know where I am if you need to talk to me.' He turned to go into his office and Rebecca followed him, closing the door behind her.

Frank gazed at her, his face softened. He had put on a brave front as a manager, but as a friend, he wanted to do so much more. She had suffered enough – if he'd had his way, he would have beaten Matt to a pulp and taken Rebecca far away from here for a month at least. But for now, he could do nothing more. 'How are you, Frey? He's shaken you up badly, I wanted to kill him.'

For a few seconds, she said nothing, and he allowed her to compose herself. He brought her some water, and she drank it gratefully. 'I hate him, Frank, I hate myself too, I nearly married him, despite my misgivings. How can one person change at a drop of a hat? I appreciate what happened to his mother was terrible, but I'm dealing with a similar thing, now that my dad has gone, and I don't behave like him, bitter and needy. They say it's not till we go through a difficult time in our lives that others can see our true colours, and I'm so glad I saw his before it was too late.

'Look at you, for example, I know I shouldn't compare you both, but when we stopped seeing each other, you behaved impeccably, you picked up the pieces and moved on with your life. You found a passion for work and threw your energies into the gym. Everything you did was positive, and you looked after yourself so well. Why can't he be at least dignified in his defeat?

'He didn't fight for me when I broke it off with him. He just defended Molly, and now he comes here, trying to humiliate us! It's made me hate him! That Molly's not right in the head either. After my dad dying in suspicious circumstances, she spies on us? And what about the strangling of Mr and Mrs Crowe's little dog? It could be Molly who did that!

'She has been circling around like a vulture to pick up the spoils, but now she's broken us up, she can have him. They deserve each other. I don't think it's dawned on her that Matt is using her for company and she panders to him – she's so childish. He just likes the attention. I don't think he is even attracted to her.' She smiled 'She's going to get an almighty shock when she finds out! I'd love to see her face when that happens.'

Frank allowed her to get it out of her system, sometimes she withheld her views, so he was glad she had opened about it. Her eventual smile reassured him, he had been so worried about her. When she smiled, his heart melted. 'Well done, Frey, for getting it all off your mind. Everything you say is spot on. Just make sure you keep your distance from Matt. Don't text, call or visit him, and if he contacts you, ignore him.'

'Don't worry, I won't. The less I see of him, the better! Anyway, I'll get back to work, at this rate, I'll get nothing done today.'

He nodded, she got up to leave, but as she started to open the door he added, 'Oh one more thing, Frey.'

She turned around to look at him, 'Yes?'

'Would you like to have dinner with me?'

She stared at him – what did he mean by that? She pushed a stray lock of hair behind her ear, 'You mean like a date?'

He smiled, 'Dinner Frey, you decide what label you choose to give it.'

She thought, *God why did he smile at her that way?* He had no idea how her feelings for him were growing. Well, two can play this game. She smiled back sweetly and said, 'Let me check my diary and get back to you. I might be busy.'

He laughed, 'No you're not.'

'Ok, fine, I'm not. What sort of time? Seven?'

'We can go straight from work, have a few drinks

first, then dinner somewhere that takes our fancy? Let's be spontaneous!'

'Oh, I like that idea. I'll text my mum to tell her my plans or she will worry.'

~

Matt circled around his living room in a rage, he called Molly over to tell her what happened at Rebecca's office. He explained how he'd struggled to get Rebecca back and how they'd treated him. Molly sat and listened to him rant on, spouting obscenities about them. She couldn't calm him.

Part of her was happy Rebecca had dumped him and the other part frustrated. Matt wanting to go back to that uppity bitch, why? Why couldn't he see Rebecca wasn't his type? She'd heard about Rebecca's letter and wished it had been her that had sent it to break them up, but she hadn't. How dare that person call her ugly! They didn't know her capabilities, everyone thought she was bubbly and fun, but they didn't see her darker side. She chose to scare the living daylights out of Rebecca last night and she had been justified to do so if she was messing around with Frank more than she was admitting to! 'Well at least she'd found out Frank and that bitch kissed – and who knows what else,' thought Molly.

'... don't you think?' asked Matt.

Molly had been so lost in her own thoughts, she wasn't listening to what he was saying, she agreed with him. She wondered if he suspected how much she loved him. How from the first time she set eyes on him, all those years ago, she had pined for him. She wished he would look at her – just once at least, the way he looked at Rebecca. Even now, he didn't know she would do anything for him. He was her best friend, and she wanted him forever, no other man would do. She had to make him change his mind. As soon as the mess with Rebecca gets sorted, he will realise she is the only woman he will ever need.

An uneventful week passed by. Molly continued to support Matt, listening, sympathising and advising. She never got fed up of being there for him. At the end of the week, he asked her to come for dinner. He told her he was fed up with cooking for one and spending evenings on his own.

Molly was over the moon. Finally, she thought. She took ages choosing what to wear that evening. After much deliberation, she picked out a favourite – her pink, burgundy and black flowery playsuit.

Next, she applied more makeup than was normal for her, and to make her hair pretty, she took her curling irons to create a new style. She always wore her medium-length black hair straight, never curled. She wanted to impress Matt, and this was her chance.

When she had finished, she looked at herself in the mirror one last time to appraise her efforts. 'He will love it,' she said out loud. Grabbing her car keys, handbag and mobile phone, she left the house.

Molly never usually bothered about her appearance, she worked as an administrator for a chain of restaurants, and sometimes, she was the only one working in the small office. But tonight, she was dressed to impress. On her way to Matt's house, she became nervous. She knocked at his door and waited. She smiled when Matt opened the door. He looked taken aback, 'Wow, Molly, you look different.'

'Is that a bad thing?' She fidgeted with her hair and felt blood rush to her cheeks.

'No, no, of course not – you look great! Where's my manners? Come in.' He stepped aside to let her in. Turning his back to her, he remarked, 'You've done your hair like Rebecca's, if it was red it would be identical, can you shut the door, please? I need to check on the food.'

As he ran off towards the kitchen, he missed the look on Molly's face. She felt like he had slapped her. She went bright red, why did he have to compare her to his ex? After a moment standing there, shocked, she collected herself and joined Matt in the kitchen.

'So what are we having tonight?' Her voice was high pitched.

'Hope you like chicken curry and rice with salad. I make a great curry.'

'Yummy.'

They spent the evening laughing and talking about their wild nights out, their university days and then they spent so much time choosing a movie on Netflix that they both wanted to watch, they didn't pick anything.

At the end of the evening, Molly and Matt were giggling as they got to his front door. 'Now, Mollykins, are you sure you can drive home yourself? I can order you an Uber. I'd rather you be safe than sorry.'

By this time, they had finished two bottles of wine, and Matt drank most of it. Molly knew she may have to drive home, so she only had two glasses. She knew she was on the borderline of the drink-drive limit, and insisted she was fine.

She was frustrated that Matt hadn't made a move on her. She was in this game for the long haul.

She giggled, 'Mollykins, funny.' On an impulse, she took a chance and moved in a little closer to Matt. When she was near enough to tiptoe up to kiss him, she whispered, 'or I could stay over tonight?'

Matt sobered up in an instant. Was she propositioning him? Had she forgotten his broken engagement was still upsetting him? 'Now, now, Molly we can't go there, and you know that.' To make it less awkward he said, 'You're a cheeky little temptress, aren't you?'

She was deflated but decided she had to try again. 'Matt,' she whispered, 'Can't you see, I'm in love with you?'

He was shocked she'd blurted this out and tried to laugh it off, although he suspected she meant it. 'Now I know you've had too much to drink. Proclamations of undying love, after how many bottles of wine? You're hilarious. Let me call you an Uber, I insist.'

Molly was slightly tipsy, but not enough not to be hurt by his callous remarks. He was trying to make light of what she'd said and she became annoyed. She took a deep breath, 'Don't worry, I'm fine. I don't need an Uber. I'm a big girl and can take care of myself. Goodnight, Matt, it was a lovely evening.' She pecked him on the cheek and hurried out.

Matt barely had time to say goodbye, but he was grateful she hadn't made him say any more to spurn her unwanted advances. He shouted, 'Goodnight Mollykins, text me when you're safely home. It's raining, so drive carefully.'

She shouted back, 'Yeah, ok.'

Molly ran to her car feeling humiliated and wretched. Tears streamed down her face – Matt will never love her. She glanced over to his front door and noticed he hadn't even waited to wave her off. She sat there sobbing, too tired to think straight.

Molly didn't know how long she stayed there, maybe five or ten minutes, before she heard a tap on her window. She hurriedly wiped her tears. Through the rain and misted-up windows, Matt wouldn't be able to see her clearly but she didn't want him to look at her in this state.

Smiling back, she said under her breath, 'Thank God, he cares.'

But when she opened the door, she was surprised to see it wasn't him. 'Oh it's you. What do *you* want?'

12

An excited Detective Sargent Xavier Townsend burst in on Chief Inspector Christopher Mills, 'Chief, we've got another one! We received word from the on-call duty inspector who said there's been a murder.'

Mills looked up in confusion, 'What? Who?'

'Molly French, that bird Rebecca Reid suspected of writing the letter she received last week.'

'Molly French? When?' Mills looked stunned.

'Looks like she'd been there for hours before they found her. We need to go there now – I just came off the phone from boss man.'

'Why didn't he ring me?'

'Your phone was engaged Chief. He said to grab you and make our way there ASAP.'

The two detectives got to Matt's house, surveyed the site and ensured the crime scene procedures of preservation were implemented.

Detective Mills said, 'Xavier, will you please liaise with the crime scene manager, inform the coroner's office, tell them we require a forensic post-mortem. Then come and join me. I need to have a quick word with Matt Rook.'

'Yes, Chief,' said Townsend.

The on-call duty inspector, Bridges, came to speak to Detective Mills whilst Townsend made his phone calls, 'I am guessing Miss Molly French was killed soon after twelve-thirty this morning. They found her under the bush at around seven fifteen by a dog walker whose dog pulled him to the body – I guess it had picked up the scent. He said she must have been dead for hours because her body was ice cold.'

Detective Christopher Mills inspected Molly French, someone had stabbed her multiple times and left her for dead. They told Inspector Bridges that Matt Rook had come out to see why the police had turned up outside his house and was distraught when he saw it was Molly. He ran to the side of his home and threw up – he didn't want to talk to anyone.

Detective Mills commented, 'It's looking very similar to the murder of Matt's mother, Macy Rook. She too was stabbed and placed under this same bush near his house. It's either a copycat murder or the same person.'

Detective Xavier Townsend came to join them a few minutes later. Mills waited for Townsend, so they could talk to Matt together. Mills nodded his head, thanked

Inspector Bridges then went to the house so that they could speak to Matt.

Matt sat there like a statue. His hair was dishevelled, his eyes appeared to have sunk back into their sockets, and his skin was pale.

Mills spoke first, 'Mr Rook, sorry to hear of your loss. Can you please tell me everything about your last meeting with Miss French? I gather the two of you spent the evening together last night.'

He didn't speak, he sat on his couch staring in the distance. Detective Townsend then spoke in slightly raised tones, 'The detective asked you a question, Mr Rook. Please try to explain what happened last night.'

Without turning to look at the detectives, Matt said in a quiet voice, 'I didn't kill her, if that's what you're thinking.'

The detectives looked at each other, Mills said, 'We need to find out what happened between you last night. It's unlikely you would have killed Miss French and left her outside your own home. So, no, we don't think you killed her. Now, please, can you detail everything that happened last night?'

Matt gave up, he nodded his head gently and explained their movements the previous night. He said he felt guilty, like it was his fault that Molly was dead.

'Why do you say that?' asked Townsend.

'Because she was in love with me, I knew that, but ignored it. Last night, she said she didn't have to drive home, she suggested spending the night with me…' he faltered.

'I take it you refused her offer?' asked Mills.

'I tried to laugh it off and make light of the situation. I didn't want to lose her as a friend and I wasn't ready for a relationship, having just broken up with Rebecca. But if I had returned her advances, she would be alive today. All I could think of was my broken heart. Now, not only did I break her heart, but I also sent her to her death!' He sobbed into his hands.

Mills decided he would not get much out of Matt, so they told him to get some rest. Later that morning, the police took Molly's body for a forensic examination. The detectives drove back to the station to brainstorm ideas.

Back at the office, Mills asked, 'So who would benefit from Molly's death? Who hated her the most?'

Townsend said, 'We both know that, there's only one – Rebecca.'

'Yes, so we'll have to get a statement and alibi from her. Anyone else?'

'Well, I can't think who would choose to kill her in that manner. Matt told us she has no family, her father is unknown and her mother passed away ages ago. Apparently she was brought up her elderly grandparents, who have also died. So she was on her own, the only friends she had were Matt, some of her work colleagues and sometimes Matt's friends Puja, Sam and Rebecca.

'Don't forget, we have that suspicious letter Rebecca received last week. Forensics showed no trace of the sender. After a tipoff from Frank Pearson, saying Molly French was spying on the Reid's, we'll need to check if

Miss French's footsteps match the ones outside the Reids' residence,' said Townsend.

'Either way, we hit a closed door, because if Miss French sent the letters, she is now dead. The thing that gets me is the similarity of the two murders outside Matt Rook's house. His mother and friend both get killed outside his house in exactly the same way. There's no doubt in my mind those murders are linked.'

Mills waited for Townsend to say something. When he didn't, Mills continued, 'Matt and Rebecca are at the centre of this. Even if they didn't do it, it's got something to do with them. The assailant definitely wants to cause Matt pain, otherwise, why kill his mother and friend? My earlier hunch was right. Macy Rook's death wasn't the result of a mugging gone wrong, it was a planned murder, too!'

'So, shall we bring in Rebecca for questioning?'

'We have to.'

On Sunday morning, Rebecca got a visit from Detective Townsend. She was shaking like a leaf when he told her of Molly's death. Erin rushed to give her daughter a hug. She couldn't believe she was killed the same was that Macy was.

Rebecca took time to gather her thoughts, 'Somebody is literally murdering people around Matt and I. It all makes sense now, they must really hate us!' she sobbed.

Erin tried to console her, 'Darling, don't cry, I am here with you. We will tackle it together. Now that the police are involved, they will catch the person, I'm sure.' She stared at the detective to support her statement.

'Yes, of course, Miss Reid, we are trying to get to the bottom of it. Please, stay calm for now.'

Rebecca looked up, wiping the tears from her face. 'The next thing I know, they will kill my mum like they killed Macy, can you protect her?'

Erin looked shocked, Townsend said, 'We will do our best, of course. But the two of you must stay on guard. Lock all the doors and windows, don't open them to anyone unless they are close family or friends. Don't go out alone till we sort this out.'

Erin said pointedly, 'Then I suggest you sort this out quickly, Detective!'

'We will try. Now, Miss Reid, can you come to the station for questioning? We aren't accusing you of anything, but we do need a formal statement.'

'She isn't going.' Erin hissed.

'Mum, we need to co-operate. How else will they catch the person if they don't ask questions?'

'Well I don't like it,' said Erin.

'I don't like any of it either, but I will go with the detective. Mum, please don't tell Frank anything just yet. He will insist on coming to the station, and I don't want anyone to be close to me right now. When I have finished with the police, I will call him. They might target both of you and you're all I got left. I don't think I could cope… with… out…' She broke down again.

'Ok darling, I won't tell him. Stay calm, love.' Erin hugged Rebecca tight.

~

At the station, they took Rebecca to an interview room where she met the detectives.

Mills opened the questioning. 'Thank you for coming to the police station willingly, we appreciate this must be hard for you, Rebecca.'

She nodded.

'I know you didn't like Miss French very much, and on the strength of the anonymous letter you received, you broke off your engagement to Mr Rook. Is that fair to say?'

'Not really Detective. Yes, it's true I couldn't stand Molly, and the letter I received played a small part in my decision to leave Matt, but the blame must rest on Matt's shoulders. He wasn't very supportive of me after my father passed away. He seemed to be more concerned with partying with Molly. I know Molly was keen on him and she did everything she could to attract him, but I didn't break off my engagement because of her.'

Mills said, 'Ok, fair point.'

'How is Matt? He will be devastated,' she asked.

'To be upfront with you Rebecca, he didn't look good when I saw him earlier. I spoke to him before you came here. He rang me to tell me there had been an argument at your workplace earlier in the week. Can you tell me more?'

Rebecca looked heavenwards, 'Just when I'm feeling sorry for him, he brandishes accusations around! Did he suggest Frank or me as possible suspects?'

'No, he didn't, but he did tell me Frank threw him out of the office!'

Rebecca stuck her chin up and said, 'Well he did kind of ask for it. If you want the story from my angle, I'd be happy to tell you.'

She explained what happened that day and how they'd had to use force to get rid of him.

Mills asked, 'Do you think Frank was too aggressive with Matt?'

'Not really, Matt was being aggressive and threatening towards the staff, to say nothing of making a fool of himself. As office manager, Frank had no choice but to throw him out. He gave him plenty of chances to control himself and discuss things sensibly, but Matt had lost it.'

'Are you two seeing each other, Rebecca? Frank and yourself?'

Her eyes widened in surprise 'No, of course not. Yes, we kissed once, the night that Molly was lurking around, but that was all. Neither of us want to start up anything so close after my broken engagement to Matt.'

'I guess *you* don't, but Frank may want to start something up. Didn't he try to break off your engagement to Matt once?'

The blood rushed to Rebecca's cheeks, 'He didn't try to break it off, he was trying to reason with Matt. Now knowing how childish Matt can be, I can see Frank was right. Yes, Frank has feelings for me, I don't think they ever went away. I guess he tried to get rid of them, but we work together, so it must have been hard for him. He has been a complete gentleman to both my mother and I, so please don't think he is underhand. He really isn't.' She was breathing hard, trying to keep her feelings in check.

'I heard he paid for your father's funeral, and supported you through it. So, from my perspective, he has invested a lot in you, emotionally and financially.'

Rebecca raised her voice, her cheeks were still red, 'What do you mean?'

'Do you think he would do anything to ease your burdens Rebecca?'

'Yes why, that's what friends do, don't they? I am so grateful to him.'

Mills whispered just loud enough for her to hear, 'Anything?'

'Yes, anything.' She blurted, then realising what he meant, she hastily added, 'I mean anything that's not illegal of, course. Please, Detective, Frank wouldn't hurt a fly. Why would he risk imprisonment for me?'

'I don't know Rebecca, would he?'

'No way, he has a sensible head on his shoulders.'

'Do you think he is "*hot-headed*"?'

'No, he is not. Now, if you've got nothing else to

ask me, then please can I go? I'd suggest you speak to Frank if you want to find out more.' She snapped.

'A few more things please Rebecca.'

She fiddled with her hair, 'Ok, go on.'

'Did Miss French ever try to contact you about Matt? Ask you to leave him or behave awkwardly towards you?'

'She never asked me to give him up, but a few times, she implied she'd spent the night at Matt's house. I don't think they were up to anything though. I think Matt was still committed to me. But she knew what she was doing, and what she wanted, and she didn't mind playing a dirty game to get him. I feel sad about it, really sad. She tried so hard to get Matt, and now she is dead and didn't even have time to be with him.'

'Ok, thanks. One last thing from me Rebecca, can you tell me where you were last night, from ten onwards?'

She didn't hesitate, 'At home, you can ask my mother. We watched some TV, nothing in particular. Then my mum went to bed. Because it was a Saturday night, I didn't want to sleep early. I think she went to bed at eleven thirty and I around one, but I'm not sure. I can assure you, as much as I disliked Molly, I don't think I've got it in me to kill anybody!'

The detective said, 'Sorry, but we needed to ask.'

She nodded, she understood he was just doing his job.

Mills looked at Townsend, 'Have you got any questions for Miss Reid, Detective?'

'Not for now.'

Detective Mills ended the interview and thanked her for her time.

~

A few days later, Rebecca called Matt to offer her condolences. She didn't really feel like talking to him, but did her duty and made the call. Frank, as expected, was shocked at the turn of events. He became even more protective towards Rebecca and Erin.

Frank accompanied Rebecca home, stayed as long as he could before going home, and he promised to text her as soon as he was home to reassure her he was safe too. They were all on high alert.

The detectives called Rebecca to tell her that the footprint analysis showed that they didn't belong to Molly French. She enquired whether they had anything else on Molly's murder.

Detective Mills said, 'There isn't much I'm allowed to say, but I can tell you this, there were stun gun marks found on Molly similar to the ones found on your father.'

Rebecca was now anxious – who would be next? The last person she feared for was herself, she was more concerned about her mother and Frank. How long could this go on for? Now they had to find who was behind it. She confided in Puja over the phone, she didn't feel happy about meeting her in person. Rebecca was scared she would endanger her friend if they met.

Puja protested, 'Don't be silly, Bec, who would want to hurt me?'

'Please, Puja, if something happened to you, I wouldn't be able to forgive myself.'

Finally, Puja relented, and they spoke almost every day instead of meeting. Puja was happy knowing Frank was always around to keep an eye on them.

Nearly a week after Molly's murder, Rebecca asked Frank for a day off on Friday. She didn't want to face another day at the office, constantly worrying about her mother, and she felt bad that Frank was not having a proper life because of her problems. For all she knew, this could go on for a very long time.

Frank said, 'Don't be silly Frey, they will find the guy. It's only a matter of time, just you wait and see. I love spending time with you, you're not stopping me from living my life, trust me.'

She gave Frank half a smile.

He said, 'Take as much time as you need – everyone in the office is worried about you. They're on edge, just know we all love and care for you.'

'I gathered that, I'm so grateful Frank. They have mothered me all week, but I need to be out of the spot-light for a little while. Will you tell them I'm fine and just need a bit of space?'

'Of course, Frey,' he said, putting an arm around her shoulders. He hadn't kissed her since the night that Molly had spied on them.

On Friday, Erin and Rebecca baked a cake to take their mind off things. Rebecca hadn't laughed so much in such a long time. She finally understood what her father had meant when he'd said that Erin was the worst baker – she was untidy, there was flour everywhere and the funniest part was when they finally took it out of the oven – it was the flattest cake Rebecca had ever seen!

She shouted, 'Mother, God almighty!'

Erin ran into the kitchen worried, but what she saw made her instantly laugh. Rebecca stood holding a burnt, flat, miserable-looking cake, giggling uncontrollably.

Rebecca put the cake on the kitchen top, so she could clutch her stomach, both women unable to talk as they laughed at their efforts.

She finally said, 'Mum, I've baked before, and it's never come out like this. It's your fault, you kept putting in more sugar than we needed!'

Erin just nodded in agreement, still chuckling 'Your dad always said I was no *Nigella Lawson*!'

They laughed even more at that whilst Rebecca tried to salvage the flat unappealing cake. Just then Rebecca's phone rang. She glanced at the number, it was unknown, so she stopped laughing and answered it whilst looking at her mum. She smiled when she recognised Frank's voice. Covering the speaker, she mouthed, 'It's Frank.'

Erin nodded, and watched as her daughter's smile faded.

Next Rebecca yelled, 'They can't do that! I will ring your uncle. Hang tight, we'll get you out of there!'

She put the phone down, deep in thought. She forgot about the cake or her mother standing there.

Erin furrowed her eyebrows, 'What's happened, dar-ling, is Frank ok?'

Snapping out of her stupor she said, 'No, he isn't. The police have taken him in for questioning. He rang me from the station, he said they may have evidence that he murdered Molly!'

13

They took Frank to the interview room where he met with both the detectives, Mills and Townsend.

Detective Mills spoke, 'Mr Pearson, you have been brought in for questioning because we need to get answers only you can give. We have interviewed a few of your work colleagues, Miss Rebecca Reid, Mr Matt Rook and a few others, and we would obviously like your statement too. This is routine for now, so nothing for you to worry about. We aren't charging you with anything – yet.' Mills stared at Frank as he spoke. Frank was motionless.

They offered him the right to a solicitor, but he waived it as he hadn't been formally charged.

After the formalities were over, Detective Mills asked Frank, 'Can you tell me your whereabouts on the night of Molly French's murder?'

Happy to co-operate, he answered, 'Yes, I was at home in my apartment. I didn't go out at all.'

'Did you speak to anyone or even on FaceTime who can vouch for you that night? They could have recognised your surroundings.'

'Not really, Detective.'

'It's safe to say you don't exactly have a great relationship with Matt Rook because of your feelings for Miss Reid, am I right?'

Frank shuffled in his chair. Detective Mills could tell Frank was a man who liked being in control. When people like him were questioned formally in the police station, they told the truth quickly to get out. The psychological manipulation had begun before he even talked.

'You are correct, I don't like Matt Rook. He is an immature, foolish boy who didn't deserve Rebecca. Although she and I haven't been romantically together for a long time, we have always remained friends and colleagues. I guess the feelings I had for her lay dormant, but lately, with all the confusion, they have come back and stronger than before. I haven't told her this because I don't want to frighten her off. I haven't even told my uncle, and I tell him everything. My priority is for Rebecca to be safe, so I prefer to stay by her side till you catch the person who has done this.'

'Thank you for being so honest, Mr Pearson,' said Detective Mills. 'Did you quarrel with Mr Rook when you found out Rebecca and he were engaged?'

'Yes, I did, but I didn't go to Matt's house with that

intention. I needed to be sure he was doing the right thing at that time and not because he had recently buried his mother. It seems my misgivings turned out to be correct.

'When I got there, he shouted at me. I think he was jealous that Rebecca had refused to give up her work, and maybe he had other issues, you'll have to ask him why he dislikes me. But I never wanted to break them up. I wanted what was best for her, and I honestly thought they were wrong together, I wanted them to see that, especially her.'

Townsend said, 'Wouldn't you say that any man Rebecca had picked would be unacceptable in your eyes because he wasn't you?'

Frank straightened up abruptly, 'Well you could say that, but I wanted the best for Frey, and if she was genuinely in love with someone, and felt that person was right for her, I wouldn't stand in her way. All I know is that Matt wasn't the man for her.'

'So, you impeded their relationship?' asked Mills.

'No, I bloody didn't, I believe it was Molly who was being underhand. In the beginning, when I found out that Mrs Rook had died, I was supportive to Rebecca, but Matt's behaviour during that period affected her badly. That's when my ears pricked up to problems in their relationship. So, when I discovered they had gotten engaged, I was sure it was the wrong thing to do. Again, it seems that I was right.' He smiled for good measure.

Townsend asked, 'Can you tell us why you argued

with Mr Rook in your offices a week before Miss French's murder?'

'What does that have to do with Molly?'

Mills snapped, 'Please Mr Pearson, just answer the question.'

'Fine, keep your hair on!' Frank told them what had happened in his office from his perspective. He said he thought Matt was either drunk or had taken drugs that day because he was irrational and had forgotten that Rebecca wasn't his fiancé anymore.

'Did you beat him up, Mr Pearson?' asked Detective Mills.

'No, of course not, I grabbed him and threw him out of the office and then my uncle came to make sure I was ok. When my back was turned, Matt attempted to punch or hit me. My uncle yelled for me to watch out, and that's when I turned and saw him charging at me. I elbowed him before he could injure me. Did he say I beat him up?' Frank smiled.

'What's so funny, Mr Pearson?' asked Townsend.

Frank tried to stifle his laugh, 'He is such a wimp! If an elbow to his chest is beating him up, then he really doesn't know the meaning of the word!'

The two detectives glanced at each other and grinned. Then Detective Mills looked serious and said, 'When we interviewed Miss Reid, she said you would do anything for her. Is the correct, Frank?'

He stopped laughing and had a faraway look, 'I realise I could be implication myself under these circumstances, now that Molly has been killed, but yes,

I would do anything for Rebecca, but pointless killing isn't one. What reason would I have to kill Molly? Just because she spied on us kissing? That's hardly a motive for a murder is it?'

The detectives said nothing about what his motive might be in killing Molly. Detective Townsend then asked, 'If you had to point a finger at who might be responsible, who would you say it was that killed Mrs Rook and Molly?'

Frank rubbed his chin, deep in thought, then said, 'Gosh Detectives, I can see you have a difficult job in front of you. I don't know who would want to see either of them dead. Obviously, someone who doesn't like Matt – that's why they're making him suffer, but don't forget that same person could well have killed Mr Reid and Lucy the dog. I suspect they are linked. But I don't know who could have done all this and why.' He raked his fingers through his hair in frustration.

The detectives continued to question him about his work life, his relationships with his staff, uncle, Erin Reid and his daily routine. After what felt like a day in the interview room, they gave Frank permission to go, but warned him not to leave the area. He agreed and was pleased to be released.

Rebecca was waiting for him and he was so glad to see her. She gave him a tight hug and directed him into her car.

'I called your uncle, and he should be in London by tomorrow midday. That was the earliest he could make it. He wasn't happy you spoke to the police without your legal representative. So, be warned, he might pounce on you when he sees you!'

'Frey, don't worry, I can handle him.'

As they got into Rebecca's car, Frank asked, 'Are you taking me home? I am so tired, all I want is a shower and sleep.'

'Yes, I am. I brought you a sandwich and some fruit, so eat. Then you can shower and sleep, it's midnight.'

'And what about you?'

'What about me? I'll drop you home and go back to mine. Do you think I will go out partying?'

'No, I mean drive home in the dark all alone? Can't you stay over with me tonight?'

Rebecca raised her eyebrows.

Frank hastily added, 'No, no, not like that. Just sleep on my bed – I can take the couch. I can't let you go back alone. It's not safe. Please, Frey,' he begged.

'Oh, all right, I'll stay. Let me call my mum as soon as we get to yours. I hope she'll be ok on her own.'

'Tell her to lock everything and not to open the door for anyone and to keep her phone charged and next to her. You both should do this every evening.'

'Wow, Frank, you say that every night you leave us, do you know that?'

'Yes, I do, and there is no need to be poke fun at me. I just worry about the two of you.'

'I know, I'm sorry. So, what did the police ask you?'

'Can I tell you tomorrow? My brain is so fried.'

'Yes, of course you can.'

Matt was annoyed when he found out that Frank hadn't been arrested for Molly's murder. He went to the station to confront the detectives. They told him they couldn't arrest Frank just because he wanted them to.

'But what about the fight he had with me? And he chased after Molly when she spied on them kissing that night.'

'If you saw someone outside your house wouldn't you want to find out who they were? And wouldn't you chase them off too? Especially at night. Molly was your friend, we get that but, she had no business going to spy on them. It isn't a reason to charge Frank with murder,' said Mills.

'Well, I don't trust him!'

'You may or may not trust anyone Mr Reid, but that won't get me to arrest him, just based on your opinion,' stated Mills.

Matt spoke louder even than he expected, 'I think you should arrest him and be done with it. He is the culprit, I'm sure of it.'

'Mr Rook, I'm afraid you need to leave, we need to do our jobs without interruptions and unfounded accusations,' said Townsend.

Matt's face was red, his eyes bulging, and he raised his voice to nearly a shout, 'It's not unfounded!'

Detective Mills looked at Townsend, he took a deep breath in trying not to lose his temper too, 'Mr Rook, please leave, we will be in touch as soon as we have more information on Miss French. You will be the first to know.'

'Ok, I'm not getting anywhere here, so I'm leaving. And let me know if you do find the assailant! And hurry up, this killing spree makes the police look incompetent!'

With that, he turned on his heels and quickly left. It was still early Sunday evening. He wanted to speak to Rebecca. He had to make her see that Frank killed his mum, Molly, and he had something to do with killing her dad too!

After leaving the police station disgruntled, he drove to Rebecca's house. He sat in his car waiting, he was unsure whether he should to speak to her after his last encounter with her. Half an hour passed, he made up his mind. If he said nothing, and she got hurt somehow, he would never forgive himself, so he unbuckled his seat-belt, walked over and knocked on her door.

After a long wait, he heard Rebecca on the other side of the door, 'Who is it?'

'It's me, Matt. Bec, please open the door. I need to speak to you.'

He heard several clicks whilst she unlocked it. Standing there, were both mother and daughter. Rebecca said, 'What do you want, Matt?' She sounded cold.

'Please can I come in, Bec?'

Rebecca and her mother exchanged glances. Erin nodded, so Rebecca stood back to let him in. When they were seated, Erin asked, 'How are you coping Matt? It must be difficult for you. Having two terrible events outside your house?'

He swallowed hard, there was a lump in his throat, 'It has been tough. It brought back the awful memories of those dark days after my mum died in that same spot. I sometimes wonder how I cope.' He stared at the floor as if there was something interesting on the carpet.

'How are your aunt and uncle? I think you should go to Manchester to see them for a while. I don't think it's safe being alone at home, and it will stop you from being lonely,' said Erin.

'They have already suggested that. But I'm waiting for the police to find the culprit first, and then I'll go. In the meantime, my aunty will come over in a few days to stay with me until I'm ready. I'm looking forward to that, so don't worry about me, Erin.' He gave her a weak smile.

Rebecca wasn't softening as quickly as Erin, 'Why are you here Matt? I'm not coming back to you, so please don't ask.'

'I haven't come to ask you to back, so you don't need to snap at me, I wanted to let you know they have released Frank from police custody. You might already know this so...'

Rebecca didn't let him finish his sentence, 'Yes, I do know, I picked him up last night and took him home.'

He looked at her like she'd slapped his face. Then he glanced at Erin, unsure what to say next.

'Ok, fine, he is out, but I'm here because I'm worried about you Bec, the police have found nothing to link him with the murder, I am sure they will, but until they do and have him safely under arrest, I don't want you anywhere near him. He could hurt you next Bec.'

He looked frantically from Erin to Rebecca, hoping they were heeding his warning. And then Rebecca did something unexpected – she laughed at him saying, 'Matt you have a vivid imagination! Frank would never hurt me.'

Matt was struggling to remain in control, he could feel his pulse start to race, 'Please Bec, he is dangerous. I don't trust him.'

'Is there anything else you need, Matt? If not, I would like you to go.'

Matt stood up, he was letting his temper get the better of him, despite warning himself earlier to keep it in check. 'What is wrong with you Rebecca?' he shouted, 'I can't believe you're the girl I fell in love with! I try to look out for you, but you don't care. It's like you've got a death wish!'

Both ladies stood up, Erin said, 'Rebecca asked you to leave, so you'd better leave. I won't have shouting in my house. Please go.'

'Erin, can't you see Frank is dangerous? He killed my mum, now Molly. Next, it could be either one of you!'

Rebecca had had enough, she raised her voice too, 'Matt, I need to make it clear to you that I don't need your protection. I'm sorry, but let's face it, you couldn't protect your mother or Molly, so it's hardly likely you'd be able to prevent anything happening to us. We are not together anymore, and you are being intimidating. I'm warning you now Matt, if you come anywhere near me uninvited again, I will get a restraining order!'

He walked towards the door, shouting, 'I've had enough of this, don't come running to me when you need my help!'

He went quietly, not looking back at them, he felt a fool coming here now. Rebecca followed closely behind him shouting, 'Running back to you? I don't think so Matt!' With that, she slammed the door on him.

An hour later, she had calmed down enough to phone Frank and tell him about Matt's visit. It enraged him, 'Oh my God, I'll give that boy the beating of his life. How dare he come over like that! Did either of you feel threatened?'

'Not really, we can hold our own. I told you not to worry about us, didn't I?'

'Frey, I have every right to worry, there is a crazy person out there trying to wreak havoc and you want me to stay calm? The police have already lost valuable time. If they'd linked all the murders earlier, we wouldn't be here. They're wasting time talking to me, they need to find who did this, and quickly.'

Rebecca tried to simmer him down, 'They will, don't worry. We need to just let it go and give them the answers we have. They will make the connection or get a breakthrough soon enough.'

'Ok, but I am still not happy about Matt. Tomorrow, I'm going over there to give him a piece of my mind, and by the time I finish with him, he will never bother you again. Just you wait and see.'

Rebecca's heart beat faster, she broke out into a mild sweat, 'Hmmm… I don't think that's a good idea. He will call the police and you could get arrested again.'

'I went in voluntarily for questioning, not because they arrested me!'

'Whatever, please Frank, don't bother with him. I've already told him if he comes harasses me again, I will get a restraining order.'

'Don't worry Frey, I won't do anything bad, just frighten him a bit. Trust me, he won't come anywhere near you again.'

'No please Frank, I will talk to him and tell him to stay away. If I speak to him nicely, he will listen, I'm sure of it.'

'Frey, are you crazy? No way.'

'I will go with my mum, so I won't be alone. He respects her, and he is harmless. He's nothing but a lot of hot air. I also want him to hurry up and go to his aunt and uncle's place in Manchester. It's only two-and-a-half hours on the train from London, so he can come back down if there's a breakthrough on the case. I think he's going stir crazy in that house all alone.'

'He should be working,' said Frank.

'Matt gave that up when his mum died, they have a lot of money. His dad left them debt free, no mortgage to pay and tons of money in the bank. What is there to work for?'

'Hmmm… but it's still making him mad doing nothing. Now with Molly gone, he will continue to harass you.'

'No, I will speak with him tomorrow. I want to take a few days off work anyway, so please?' Rebecca begged.

'Ok, let's discuss it tomorrow, eh? I'm going out to dinner with my uncle tonight. Would you both like to join us?'

'No thanks Frank, you enjoy his company for a change. You hardly get to see him. I'm sure you two have a lot to talk about. Mum invited Puja and Sam to come round and we will have a takeaway. I would ask if you wanted to come over, but you've got plans too – So, it's kind of worked out well.'

'Ok, great, I'll call you tomorrow, and I will definitely text you later.'

Rebecca suddenly had a warm feeling in her body, 'Yes, I know you will.'

She smiled as she disconnected the call but then the smile faded. She knew what she had to do, and it involved Matt.

14

'So, what do we know so far?' asked Detective Mills.

The two detectives decided it was time to put their cards on the table and look at what they were dealing with. They wanted to eliminate or focus on key suspects.

Detective Townsend said, 'Ok, let's take it from the start, with Mrs Rook's murder.'

'No, let's concentrate on Miss Molly French and see if we can connect her with the others.'

Townsend preferred to work from the first case and work through each one in order, but he knew his method took time, and they needed to wrap this case up, 'Fine, ok let's begin with Miss French. On the day of her murder, she went to Matt's house for dinner. From what we gather, she thought it was a date, and was excited about it.

'She has a nice dinner, they don't pick a movie to

see because they had fun just choosing what they wanted to watch and had been drinking wine. At around twelve midnight and with a little alcohol in her system, she left. She makes a pass at Matt, which he rejects, she goes to her car but doesn't drive off.

'The next information is extrapolated from what we find out after she gets killed. We are assuming she doesn't get forcibly removed from her car because there aren't signs of damage or struggle. That means she got out her car to talk to someone she recognised. Matt said he was tipsy and didn't see Miss French again until he saw her body the next day. So, she didn't get out her car for Matt but for someone else she knew.'

Mills interrupted, 'Yes, because if it was a stranger, she would have wound her window down, not physically got out the car. There's no good reason to suspect Matt because he wouldn't have invited Miss French to his house and then kill her right outside. Plus, he would never have killed his mother too, by all accounts, it devastated him when she died. So, we can rule him out of the equation.'

'Yes, I agree, he's out. So now we're back to Miss French who got out of the car for someone she knew. She talks to the person, and at some point, they attack her. The bush they dragged her to, was ten feet away. Her body had only been moved three feet, so she must have walked with her assailant...'

'Or they coerced her,' said Mills.

'Yes, they could have got her to walk towards the bush. Then attacked her and dragged her under it, and left her to bleed out from her wounds. From the forensic examination, we've found out they had stunned her with a gun similarly to Mr Reid, but unlike him, they stabbed her five times. The assailant had definitely wanted her dead.

'She died from her wounds within five to ten minutes. There were no witnesses at that hour of night. Miss French's car door was closed, so I can only assume she wanted to talk to the person she got out of the car for. All ok so far?'

'Yes absolutely,' said Mills. 'There were no footprints we could take from the crime scene because it had rained all night. Whatever was there was washed away, and from what the team have reported, they think the murderer smoothed off some prints manually – it wasn't as wet under by the bush, so there should have been footprints there, but there weren't.'

Townsend replied, 'Yeah, so no footprints. The stun gun links Miss French's murder to Mr Reid, and the location of the murder, in a copycat fashion, links to the murder of Mrs Rook too.'

'Uh huh,' said Mills, nodding his head. His eyes were firmly cast on the floor whilst he was thinking.

They both walked around Mills' office whilst they went through their thought processes.

Then Townsend said, 'So now let's talk about the suspects one at a time.'

Mills nodded again, so Townsend continued, 'First let's start with Mr Pearson. He admits to being in love with Rebecca Reid. We have to eliminate him from the murder of Miss French because, although he has no alibi, he didn't seem that flustered when he told us he'd been at home alone all night. We've got CCTV footage from the garage of his building to confirm he didn't move his car out of his parking lot. Now, he may have got a lift or walked then taken a taxi, but he didn't. We received information from his mobile phone company that he was using his Wi-Fi and his IP address matches his home address.'

Mills agreed, 'Yes, so that rules him out of Miss French's murder, and he had no motive to murder Mrs Rook or even Mr Reid.'

'Plus, on the day of Mr Reid's murder, Mr Pearson was in his office,' said Townsend.

'So, on those facts, Frank Pearson can be ruled out.'

'Yup, so who have we got left, apart from Rebecca and Erin Reid?' asked Townsend.

'What about any of Mr Pearson's staff or Mr Logan Pearson?' suggested Townsend.

'No, no joy there either. There were no motives at all. And Mr Pearson has an alibi, he was in Scotland for all the offences, so we can forget about him. Ok, let's talk about Erin next.'

'Erin Reid was home on the night that Miss French died. Rebecca was home too, and neither of them saw each other from eleven-thirty till breakfast the next day.'

'If she did it, she would have brought a stun gun – that she had from stunning Mr Reid before – and a knife and driven over to Matt's house. Even if she had left at eleven-thirty, or if she arrived there at midnight, she would have had to wait outside for Miss French to come out. Unless she intended to attack Matt Rook and chose Miss French instead because she was an easy target. But that doesn't check out either because didn't we get an alibi for Mrs Reid when her husband was killed?' asked Mills.

Detective Townsend shuffled around with the papers and files on the desk, 'Yes, I think we did, hang on, let me check for sure.' After a minute of scanning through a few files, he declared, 'Ah yes, here it is. She took a taxi to the shopping centre and was spotted on CCTV and identified by shop staff too. So, she has a watertight alibi.'

'And she had no reason to kill Mrs Rook, so she is definitely out. Now Rebecca, let's look at her motives and alibi,' said Mills.

Townsend sighed heavily, 'Right, yes, Miss Rebecca Reid. She has a powerful motive for killing Molly French, she had no alibi, so she could have killed her, but not Mr Reid. She was at work when he was murdered. And she doesn't have a good motive for killing Mrs Rook, so I guess she's out too.'

'Unless…' Mills said, putting his finger up in a Poirot-style gesture. Townsend raised his eyebrows. '… unless we are looking at two people! What if Rebecca killed Molly French the same way Mrs Rook and her father were murdered, but someone else killed Mrs Rook and Mr Reid?'

'Ah, let's discuss that possibility. If we assume Rebecca killed Miss French, then we can rule out Erin

Reid and Frank Pearson, as they both also have alibis for Mr Reid. What if Molly French killed Mr Reid? She could have murdered both Mr Reid and Mrs Rook, but I fear we are clutching at straws here. What would her motive be? It's all too confusing!' Townsend scratched his head in frustration.

Detective Mills walked around the office again and again, deep in thought then said, 'There must be a factor or individual we haven't considered. We need to delve into the past. See if there is someone connected to Matt Reid. Someone that wanted to hurt him, someone angry enough to murder his mother and friend. Not sure about Mr Reid, but there may be a connection apart from him just being Rebecca's dad.'

Townsend's eyes lit up, 'Yes, let's look at other possibilities. And another thing, what if the person that killed Mrs Rook had actually come to kill Rebecca that day but encountered her father instead and so killed him?'

Mills said, 'Yes, there are so many possibilities so we need to dig into their past lives. Both Matt Rook and Rebecca Reid, they are connected somehow, they have to be.'

They both seemed happy that they had eliminated a few suspects, but now they had more work to do and needed to find the culprit before anyone else got murdered. It was imperative they worked fast.

The next few days passed by quickly, they checked Matt's last place of employment to see if there had been any disputes with either management or his colleagues, but they all consistently praised him for his hard work and good sense of humour. There were no ex-girlfriends that had a grudge against him. Apart from Rebecca and his friend Molly, he had only seen one other girl who had now moved to America so that ruled her out. Everywhere they looked, when it came to Matt Rook, was a closed door.

Whilst Mills was trying to find out information about Matt Rook, Townsend dug up Rebecca Reid's past, and in a similar fashion, he didn't come up with much. Nobody really hated her enough to kill her dad, so that brought them back to having no real answers to their many questions.

By the end of the week, both the detectives were getting fed up and frustrated with their efforts. Nothing was making sense or appeared to be going right for them. On the Friday night, they decided to relax – Mills suggested they mull over the few bits of information they'd gleaned through the week at his house, over a pizza and beer. Townsend gratefully accepted. It had been a tough week, and they needed to slow the pace for a night.

After the pizza, they took another look at the facts. Although Xavier enjoyed Chris's company, he could feel a headache coming on and thought maybe an early night might be in order. But now, he had to put his thinking cap back on and rehash all the information about their case, his head began to throb.

Christopher looked at him, 'What's the matter, Xavier? You look tired, hope you're not coming down with something.'

Rubbing his forehead, he said, 'I've got a headache, Chris, have you got any paracetamol?'

'Yes, of course. Ok, don't drink any more beer, I'll make you a nice mug of tea.'

Xavier was grateful, he'd always liked Christopher Mills. Whilst Christopher was in the kitchen, he put his head back on the couch and closed his eyes to soothe the pain in his head. He heard Chris's mobile phone ring but didn't look at it. He would tell Chris it had rung when he came back with his tea.

But a minute later, his own phone rang, and he picked it up. It was the station, he listened for a few seconds and said, 'That's because he couldn't hear it. We're at Detective Mills' house having a pizza and looking over the case.'

He listened for a few more seconds and got up in a flash, Christopher came into the living room with the tea and tablets, he looked at Xavier's face, he had finished his conversation and was holding his phone in his hand, he appeared to be miles away.

'Xavier, mate, here is your tea, and take the pill. Did my phone ring – I thought I heard it, and why are you standing there like that?'

Xavier snapped into the present, 'Erm… that was the station. They tried you first, and when you didn't pick up, they called me. We've got to leave, there's been a fire!'

'What, where?'

'At Matt Rook's house, like the whole place is up in flames, and they suspect he's inside. We've got to go now, the fire service is already at the scene.'

'Ok, ok, let's hurry. I'll put on my shoes and get my car keys. You swallow those tablets with some tea – I can't see your headache getting any better without them – it will be a long night!'

15

M att Rook's house was an inferno by the time the two detectives got there at eleven-thirty. They were told that someone had called the fire department at about eleven, before the fire had engulfed the house, as it did now. There were neighbours, onlookers, firefighters and the police.

They had evacuated the neighbours to the right and left of Matt's house as the firefighters worked to tackle the blaze. The police had cordoned off much of the area. Mills was shocked at the ferocity of the fire.

'This doesn't look like a normal house fire, Xavier. There is definitely foul play.'

Townsend nodded, his headache had receded but not left him yet. He hoped Matt Rook wasn't home, and the perpetrator hadn't wanted to cause him harm. If he had been home when the fire took hold, he would never survive this blaze.

After talking to residents, they found that nobody knew about the fire till fire service was called. There was nothing more they could do. The Forensic Unit had to attend the site, and the fire team had to send in their report. Mills said to Townsend, 'I want the whereabouts of both the Reid ladies and Mr Logan as soon as possible. I've had enough of this shit! If Matt Rook was in the house, and it's proved that he perished in that fire, I will leave no stone unturned, I'm telling you now! What you are seeing is the nice Detective Chief Inspector, but I will go nuts at every witness, or possible witness I have to interview! Somebody is hiding something, and I want it stopped.' He was breathing hard.

Even Detective Townsend hadn't seen this side of him. He was upset too. After all the work they'd put into this case, it felt like the murderer was laughing at them.

All he could say was, 'Yes boss. Don't worry about it today. Let them do their jobs, we can find out all the facts tomorrow.'

The next day, Erin woke Rebecca. Rebecca had been trying, unsuccessfully, to sleep in. Her phone kept buzzing message alerts, but she'd tried to ignore them, deciding to pick them up later. But now, her mother was banging on her door, and she gave up, 'What do you want, Mum?' she called irritably. 'It's seven-thirty on a Saturday morning! What does a girl need to do to get some sleep around here?'

Her mum barged in, 'Rebecca, wake up, there's been a fire at Matt's house last night. Puja rang to tell me because she couldn't get hold of you!'

'What? Is he ok? Did Puja speak to him?' She sat up quickly, rubbing her eyes.

'She doesn't know what's happened to him, he isn't answering his phone. Puja called the police to glean information, but she's getting nowhere.' Erin took a breath and paced her room, distractedly.

Rebecca looked at her phone, she had lots of missed calls and messages from Puja, Frank and Sam. She had an awful feeling when she saw there were none from Matt.

The first person she called was Frank. If anyone could obtain information on the fire, it would be him. He picked up her call on her first ring.

'God, Rebecca, finally! Have you heard about the fire?'

'Yes, my mum just told me. Is Matt ok? Did you find out what happened?'

'I'm not sure exactly, but I watched the news on the internet and the Twitter feeds, they've classed the fire as suspicious. It was a ferocious fire. There's no news about Matt. Someone even mentioned that there was only one person living in the house and he hasn't identified himself yet.'

She fell silent.

'Frey, are you there?'

'Yes,' she whispered.

'Oh, I thought I'd been cutoff and was speaking to myself. I'll get ready and go to the police station straight away, I suggest you do too. I am sure they will want a statement from us, so we should go to them before they come calling. That way, we might find out more information about the fire too.'

'Frank…'

'Yes, what is it Frey?'

She sighed and said, 'What if he is dead in that house?'

'Now Frey, stop speculating, nothing is certain at the moment.'

'I know him Frank, he wouldn't hide like this. If he were alive, we would have seen him, he enjoys attention too much. That person wanted him dead, and they have got what they wanted!'

'Please, stop speaking this way. We know nothing for sure. When we get to the station, I will insist on twenty-four-hour protection for you and your mum. This is ridiculous! It could have been your house they burned. For all we know, that person may still try it!'

Rebecca said nothing. Then Frank continued, 'Ok, Frey, you go get showered and changed, have breakfast, and I'll come over. And tell your mum to get ready too, she will need to come with us. They'll want all our alibis for last night!'

When they arrived at the station, Detective Townsend was expecting them. Frank had called ahead to inform them they were going over to offer their statement.

Detective Mills met them inside and suggested he give them an update first, before calling them in individually.

'Thank you for coming here voluntarily, I guess you

must have questions about what went on last night. I can tell you only what I'm permitted to share with the public, which I will do shortly.

Last night, as you know, there was a huge fire at Matt Rook's house. The firefighters had a job tackling the blaze. This morning, when the fire crew secured the house, they deemed it to be suspicious!'

Rebecca gasped and covered her mouth with her hands. She said, 'And Matt?'

Mills looked at her and added, 'Yes, we are guessing someone deliberately set the house on fire with Mr Rook in it. When they got inside, they found a burnt body on the floor of the living room, with their hands behind their back. We can only assume the person to be Matt Rook, and he probably died in the position he was left in. His hands were tied with some rope or twine that burned up in the fire, leaving him in that ghastly position.'

Rebecca began silently crying, Erin felt tears in her eyes but did her best to keep them at bay, and Frank just looked uncomfortable, shuffling his feet whilst he stared at the floor. They were all silent, so Mills continued, 'We assume the body belongs to Matt because he was the only inhabitant in the house and he hasn't, as yet, checked himself in as safe. We are working to get dental records to establish a definite match. But for now, we don't have a positive identification. Or… there could be another explanation.'

'Like what,' asked Frank?

'Like, what if Matt is the culprit, trying to shift

focus off himself, and he locked his house with someone else in it to make us think it was him lying there!'

Rebecca spoke, 'God that's terrible. Matt would never do that, it was his mother's house.'

'But even you said the Matt you knew differs from what he is now,' said Townsend.

'Yes, he is, but that would mean he killed his mother too! No, I refuse to believe that about him!' She wiped the tears off her face as she considered what the detectives were suggesting.

Mills said, 'So now you have all been brought up to speed on what happened last night, I want to interview you one by one. Erin, can I start with you, please?'

Erin nodded, looking at Rebecca, 'You go, Mum. Frank is here. I'll be ok.' So Erin followed the detectives.

Once she was in the interview room, Detective Mills began the questioning, 'Where were you yesterday evening between ten and this morning?'

'At home.'

'Were you alone or with Rebecca?'

'I was alone, Rebecca said she needed to go out, she told me she had lots on her mind and she wanted to drive around to clear her head. I tried to persuade her not to leave because we were trying to stay safe but she went anyway. Now…' she trailed off.

'Now what, Mrs Reid?' asked Townsend.

'… Now I am glad she had gone out. If that madman had come to burn our house down, she would have been in it too! I can't think anymore. I used to believe we were safe at home if I locked my doors and windows, but now this!'

Townsend felt sorry for her, she was still a pretty woman, but her eyes looked tired, and the way she clasped her hands on her lap, periodically wringing them, made him feel protective towards her.

Detective Mills then spoke, 'Can you remember what time your daughter came back home, Mrs Reid?'

'I am not sure, Detective, I was in bed.' Then she hastily added, 'But Rebecca didn't do this to Matt, she is too sensitive, so she wouldn't have killed him.'

'Mrs Reid, when did you last see Matt Rook alive?'

'Oh, that would be the day he came round to warn us off Frank, the day after you questioned Frank.' The two detectives nodded, and she said, 'Yes, it was the day after that.'

'Did he seem worried about anything, apart from being angry that Frank hadn't been arrested?'

'Not really, he was focused on Rebecca and nothing else. He was very protective of her and I don't get why. When they were together, he didn't give two shits about her!'

The detectives looked at each other. They asked Mrs Reid a few more routine questions, before quickly ruling her out of their investigation and let her go.

Townsend suddenly said, 'Mrs Reid, I suggest you go home and not wait for the other two. We will interview Frank next, and it may take a while.'

'I think I'll stay with Rebecca for now.'

'As you wish.' He escorted her out and invited Frank Pearson to the interview room.

But Frank said, 'I'd prefer to go last, I don't mind waiting. Rebecca, do you want to go next?' He looked at her gently.

Detective Townsend looked annoyed, 'This isn't a debate and we aren't giving you an option. Mr Pearson, so please, can you follow me?'

Frank frowned, 'I was only thinking of Rebecca!' he muttered, but he followed him anyway.

Once in the interview room, Frank said, 'So, Detective Mills, here we are again. You think I killed that idiot, Matt, don't you?'

Mills smiled, 'Just doing our job, Mr Pearson.'

'Well, if you were doing a *good* job Matt, Molly and the others would still be alive, wouldn't they?'

The detective's smile vanished. 'Mr Pearson, you hated Matt Rook, didn't you? Did you kill him by tying him up, and torching his house last night?'

'Of course not. Why would I?'

'Because you hated him?'

Frank shuffled in his chair, contemplating what to say next, he then said, 'Ok, yes, you are correct. I couldn't stand that little bastard! He was like an irritating fly I wanted to swat. He always managed to annoy Frey, but in truth, I'd have been happier giving him a nose bleed and a black eye that he could wear with pride than killing him!'

The detectives glanced at each other and grinned at Frank's choice of words.

He continued, 'I even told Rebecca, that I wanted to go over to his house and teach him a lesson he wouldn't forget, but she talked me out of it.'

'Mr Pearson, when did you have this conversation?' asked Townsend.

'About a week ago, the day after you guys questioned me. Matt went over to see Rebecca and her mother to warn them off me. Obviously, they didn't listen to his pointless request. Eventually, Erin had to ask him to leave, and Rebecca told him if he came around or near her uninvited again, she would take out a restraining order against him.'

'And did he go?' asked Mills.

'Yes, he did, but he wasn't happy. I told Rebecca I would go to his house and give him something to remember me by, but she's a very forgiving person and persuaded me to keep away.'

'And did you?' Mills folded his arms in front of his chest.

'Yes, of course, would I be telling you I hated him or about my conversation with Rebecca if I did it?'

'You could be playing games with us, Mr Pearson. Aren't you worried that you may implicate yourself in his murder? You clearly wanted him dead!' said Mills.

Frank sat forward in his chair, 'I don't give a damn if he is alive or dead. Rebecca was getting fed up with him. 'Besides, if I had wanted to kill him, I would never do it like that, with fire.'

'Oh, really?' Detective Townsend looked surprised. 'Well, how would you do it then?'

'I'd give him a good beating first, then maybe finish him off by throwing him off a cliff or something! Look, I run a very successful business and have responsibilities to my uncle, staff and Rebecca. I have a great deal to lose. But even without all that, I could never kill someone, no matter how much I dislike them or dream about it.'

Mills then asked, 'So where were you last night? Between ten o'clock and this morning?'

'At home. I spoke to Rebecca, who told me she was tired and was going to bed. So, I had an early night too. I had a stack of books that weren't being read, so I browsed through them and chose one that took my fancy and read. I didn't last long, by eleven-thirty my eyes couldn't focus on the words, so I turned out my light and slept.'

'What time did you speak to her, Mr Pearson?'

'I guess it was just after dinner, nine or nine-thirty.'

'Did you hear from Miss Reid at all that night?'

'Not till the morning when she called me. I found out about the fire and tried to ring her several times. I was worried as she wasn't picking up.'

'When did you find out that Matt's house was on fire?'

'I got a phone call from Rebecca's friend, Puja, early in the morning, saying she'd had a notification on her phone about a local fire, so she wanted to check if everything was ok. She was worried about Rebecca and the strange deaths that were taking place around her.

When she couldn't get through to Frey, she called me. She thought I might know where she was.'

'And did you know where Miss Reid was?'

'I used to keep my phone on silent at bedtime, but due to everything that's been going on with Rebecca, I stopped doing that. I looked at my phone, but there were no messages or calls from her, so I assumed she was in bed.'

'Did you know she had gone out last night after your phone call with her?'

He raised his eyebrows, 'No I didn't, did she?'

'Yes, she did. Her mother said she went for a drive to clear her head.'

Frank fell silent, his eyes dropped to the floor. He said, 'If I'd known she wanted to go out, I'd have warned her against it!'

Then Townsend asked, 'Do you think Rebecca's capable of killing Matt Rook?'

Frank looked furious, 'Are you mad? You've met Rebecca, do you really think she'd stoop that low – start a fire? No way.'

Mills smiled, 'You have a lot of faith in her, don't you?'

'Why wouldn't I? I love her.' He stuck his chin out and looked directly at Detective Mills.

'So, you would protect her if she had killed Matt? Or could you even have helped her?'

'Detective, there's a phrase for that.'

'And what is that, pray tell, Mr Pearson?'

Detective Townsend watched this cat-and-mouse exchange with amusement.

'Clutching at straws!' Frank laughed loudly.

Detective Mills' stared hard at Frank. 'You can laugh all you want, Mr Pearson, but I will be the one that gets the *last* laugh. Trust me.'

'I'd prefer it if you caught the man that killed everyone rather than just choose any person nearby that happens to catch your eye.'

'So, what did Rebecca Reid say to calm you down that day?' Mills asked.

'She said she wanted to speak to him first. She said if she asked nicely, he would listen to her.'

'And I presume she talked to him, what did she say about that meeting?'

'Oh, I don't know. I forgot to ask her, I assume she never saw him because she always told me what happened between them, and as she said nothing, I guess she didn't meet up with him.'

Townsend asked, 'If she had, are you sure she would have told you?'

'One hundred percent, she's an all-or-nothing kind of girl!'

'And what you're suggesting is that because she didn't tell you, she couldn't have gone?'

'Yes, that's what I'm trying to say. You can ask her, but the last time she saw him was at her house when he was ranting on about not trusting me!'

'Hmm, ok, Mr Pearson, I understand. Just a few more questions, then you can go.'

Fifteen minutes later, they released him. Frank felt drained and confused. There was a trail of death, and it was all centred around Rebecca.

Back in the waiting area, he saw Rebecca, by herself, 'Where is Erin?'

'Oh, she was tired, so a female police officer took her home. She will stay with her till I get back.'

'Now, there's a thought, we need to ask them to keep a twenty-four-hour surveillance on you two. I'm worried that your mother is the next target. Oh, they told me you went out last night. Why did you do that? I told you not to go anywhere alone Frey.'

'Miss Reid, can you please follow me?'

They both stopped speaking and looked at the police officer there to escort her to the interview room. She gave Frank a weak smile. 'Ok, show-time!' She said. She didn't answer Frank's question.

'I'll wait for you Frey, see you soon, I hope.' He kissed her on the cheek, the scent of her hair and her warmth made him want to hug her, run away with her, snuggle her in his arms – everything. He struggled to focus on the situation at hand.

She could see the familiar look of longing in his eyes. Rebecca moved in closer, 'Please Frank, can you go home to be with my mum? I know we've got a lot to talk about, but we can't do it right now. I'll catch you later.' She lifted her arm to caress his cheek. He was warm, and his cheek felt rough from over a day's growth of beard.

'Hm… Miss Reid?'

They both snapped back to the present, 'Oh yeah, I'm coming,' she said, turning away from Frank, to follow the police officer.

Frank watched her go saying, 'Ok, just ring me when you're done, and I will come and collect you.'

She stole a quick backward glance at him and smiled.

He watched her as she walked. '*Oh that hair.*' God how he loved her.

16

'**M**iss Reid, thank you for coming to the station. Please take a seat.'

Rebecca gave Detective Mills a half-smile and sat where directed.

'So, this must have come as something of a shock to you, Miss Reid?' said Mills.

'Please call me Rebecca. Yes, everything has.'

'Everything?'

'Everything – Matt, Molly, my dad! My world has been turned upside down.'

'So, let's start with Matt, if you don't mind. He is the latest victim, all the details and your memories will be fresh in your head.'

She nodded her head in acceptance.

'So, Miss Reid – Rebecca, when did you last see Matt Rook?'

'He came over to our house on Sunday, after

you questioned Frank about Molly, to warn us – my mum and I – about Frank.'

'Did he say that and leave?'

She smiled, 'Not really, nothing about Matt over the last few months has been easy. He made even the most straightforward conversation difficult. I guess everything changed after his mother died. He became a different person.'

'So, what did he say that day?'

'He came in, sat with us like a gentleman then he opened his mouth.' She frowned and shrugged her shoulders.

Mills smiled saying, 'What happened when he opened his mouth?'

'The usual, more senseless rubbish. He said that Frank had killed everyone and that we should stay away from him, now he'd been released. I didn't want to hear it, so I asked him to leave.'

'Did you not believe him, Rebecca?'

'No, of course not, how could Frank kill anyone, and why? He had no reason to kill Molly and…'

Mills interrupted her, 'But he did.'

'What would that be?'

'You, Rebecca, he wanted to make your life easier. Molly was taunting you, so he killed her help you out.'

She laughed, 'That's absurd! Frank is an intelligent and professional man. Killing for a woman – any girl, isn't within his capabilities. Yes, he has the strength to do it, but he has the softest heart.'

'Setting fire to a house is easy, and if Matt was making your life difficult, couldn't he have done that?'

'He could have, but he didn't, I am sure of it.'

'So, what else did you two speak about, apart from Frank?'

'Nothing, he was getting agitated, as usual. He started raising his voice, so my mum asked him to leave. Then, before he left, he said he wouldn't help me if I was in trouble because I had burnt that bridge. Or something along those lines.'

'And that was the last time you saw him?' Mills and Townsend were observing her carefully.

'Yes, it was.' She spoke more quietly, 'The last time, ever.'

Detective Mills gave a big sigh, 'Shall we grab a quick coffee and comfort break, Rebecca?'

'Yes please, I feel stifled in this room.'

They all agreed to reconvene in fifteen minutes.

Whilst the female police officer looked after Rebecca, Detective Mills received an urgent phone call about the fire. Detective Townsend followed him to his office to find out what the new development was.

The call was from the Boris Lowe of the CCTV Forensics Unit, 'Detective Mills sir, it's Boris, I need to talk to you. Some evidence has come in from last night's fire.'

Mills nodded his head several times whilst listening to Boris on the other end of the line then said, 'Are you sure, Boris, have you made a positive ID?'

Mills nodded his head a few more times and said, 'I

see. Ok, I will deal with it. Keep working to clear it up if you can, and I will call you later. I am interviewing Miss Rebecca Reid right now.'

Detective Mills said his goodbyes and looked up at Townsend, 'Boris is attempting to clear up the street lighting. He said the glare of the low pressure sodium lighting, which produces a yellowish light, is frustrating his efforts to clear up the footage. He has a vague idea though so, we may have a small lead.'

Detective Townsend smiled, 'God, about bloody time, spill, who is it?'

When the two detectives got back to the interview room, Rebecca was sitting, her arms lent on the table and her hands cupping her face. She looked like she was miles away.

She glanced up as the door opened, 'That was a long fifteen minutes, Detectives!'

Detective Townsend spoke, 'Sorry Miss… hmm, Rebecca,' he corrected himself.

'Let's get on with it then,' she snapped, she was exhausted and starting to feel irritable.

'Rebecca, can you tell us where you were last night between ten and six a.m.?' asked Detective Mills.

'I was at home with my mum, as usual.'

Mills raised his eyebrows, 'All night?'

'Yes, more or less.'

'That's not what your mum told us.'

She shuffled in her chair, she sat on her hands to stop them from fidgeting and said nothing for a minute.

Detective Mills was a patient man, he wanted her to speak when she was ready. He could see she was deep in thought. Then he said, 'So, what's the deal? Why does your mother's story differ from yours?'

She finally spoke, 'Ok, yes, I went out for a night-time drive. I was fed up with Frank and my mum breathing down my neck all the time. I was either cooped up at home or the office. Going out with Puja, or doing normal things, like going to the movies or to a club has not been possible while some killer has been on the loose. Both Matt and I were being targeted, so I've had to lie low.

'Last night, I felt like the walls were closing in on me, so I told Frank I was retiring to bed and went for a drive. My mum didn't want me to go out either, so I told her I had to meet up with Puja.'

'But you didn't meet with her, did you?'

'No I didn't, I drove around for a while. My first intention was to go to Matt's house to warn him to stay away from us, because I knew that if I didn't say anything to him, Frank would have had a fight with him. But then I remembered, I told Matt I would get a restraining order if he came near me, so not wanting to push his buttons, I thought better of it, and decided to call him on the phone instead.'

'And did you call him?'

'I was too tired to think clearly after that, so I stopped in a Tesco car park, shut my eyes and tried to relax for a while. The supermarket was closed and the car park was empty. I felt safe because nobody was there. I'm not sure how long I stayed. Then I drove around some more, and then went back home.'

'Did you drive round to Matt's house at any point last night?'

'No, I didn't.'

'Are you sure?'

'Yes, of course. I didn't want to tell you I went for a drive because of the fire. I don't really have an alibi, I was worried you would suspect me of killing Matt.'

'But you hated Matt and Molly, didn't you?'

'Without wishing to speak ill of the dead, I couldn't stand her. I found her to be quite the conniving bitch I'm afraid. But Matt… I'm not sure, it was a bit of a love–hate relationship really. But I didn't kill him. I just don't go around killing people!'

Detective Mills decided to change the topic to put her off guard, 'Have you ever seen a stun gun, Rebecca?'

'Not really, I didn't kill my dad either, if that's what you're getting at.'

'What I'm struggling with Rebecca, is why everyone around you is dying one by one? Do you not like them?'

Her face flushed, 'Don't be silly. I loved my dad, and I couldn't have done it. I was at work anyway.'

'Yes, but Frank would cover for you. He does love you, and you said he would do anything for you. Maybe not kill, but he is capable of keeping secrets! Do you not think? Perhaps you told him you had problems at home, you killed your dad by mistake and told him to vouch for you at work!'

She was breathing harder, 'And perhaps you have an overactive imagination, Detective. Have you ever thought of writing books with those storytelling abilities of yours?'

Mills laughed to ease the tension. 'I am just trying to do my job, Rebecca. Now, did you meet Mrs Rook – Matt's mum often?'

'Only once or twice, but I told you this already.' She retorted. The detectives noticed she was becoming defensive.

'Was she nice to you, Rebecca?'

'I guess, we didn't clash or anything, if that's what you mean.'

'So, you had no reason to kill her.'

'None,' she replied calmly.

'Ok, let's talk about last night for a moment please. You said you drove around and then drove home, is that correct?'

'That's what I said, and I stopped at Tesco's and stayed there for a bit.'

'Which Tesco's is that?'

'To be honest Detective, I can't remember. All I know was that I was driving around for a while. I can't remember landmarks or where I was. I knew I wasn't too far from home. Maybe four or five miles.'

'So you could have set fire to Matt's house then drove around for a while, wouldn't that be possible?'

'It is, but I didn't do that.'

Nobody said anything for a while, then Detective Mills glanced at Townsend and said, 'Rebecca, we need to speak to you about some evidence that has come to light this morning.'

She nodded her head and looked at both the detectives in turn.

'Whilst we had a quick break earlier, I had a call from our CCTV Forensics Unit who said they've recovered footage of the crime scene from a GoPro camera that recorded what happened. The camera belongs to the neighbours opposite Matt Rook's house. They'd installed the camera quite recently, following the activity around Mr Rook's house.' He was watching her closely.

'Oh,' was all she answered.

Mills continued, 'They're examining the footage now, but before the actual fire, at around ten thirty-five pm, the camera captured someone walking towards Matt's house. Do you know who that was Rebecca?'

'No, but I have a feeling you're going to tell me.'

'The person fits your height and weight description, we even have footage of the woman – yes it was a woman – turning around to check if anyone was watching. And guess what? We got a partial view of your face and that unmistakable red hair.'

'What?'

Detective Townsend – who was playing the good cop, as agreed earlier – bent down, and coming closer to her face, said, 'I'd suggest you tell us everything,

Rebecca.' His voice was calm and gentle. He was trying to coax a confession out of her.

'I told you everything. That woman isn't me.' She started sweating, her heartbeat felt erratic, and she fiddled with her hair.

'But you admit to being out last night, don't you Rebecca?'

'Yes, I do, but I went nowhere near Matt's house.'

'You said you can't remember where you drove.'

'I can't remember places I haven't been to before, but I would remember if I'd been to his house. You said that the woman was walking towards Matt's house, and I'm sure that it wasn't me. I didn't get out of my car. I'm sure of that.'

Detective Mills suddenly banged his fist on the table, startling her and Townsend equally. 'Damn it Rebecca, tell us the truth! Did you set fire to Matt's house last night?'

Rebecca sobbed.

Mills shouted at her, 'Tell me the truth, and this will all be over.'

She screamed back, 'I am telling you the fucking truth! I don't know how that woman could be me, it's not me. I am a hundred percent sure it isn't.'

Detective Townsend calmed her down, 'Rebecca,' he whispered, 'maybe you went there but blanked the whole thing from your mind?'

She wiped the tears from her face with a tissue she found in her pocket, 'It's possible that I may have blanked driving past Matt's house, but I couldn't have blanked setting fire to anything. I had no lighters or matchboxes in my car. I don't even smoke. Even if I'd had a moment of madness and decided to set fire to his house, I would have needed a lighter on me, which I don't. Plus, I would have needed some kind of accelerant, then go inside, tie Matt up, then start the fire. I couldn't do all that and not remember. I can't even think it, let alone do it!' she wailed.

The two detectives looked at each other, they gave her some time to compose herself and stepped outside the interview room.

Detective Townsend said, 'Could she be telling the truth, Chief? Didn't you say Boris said the footage was grainy?'

'Well, if not her, then who?'

'What about her mother? They left her all alone in the house. She is the same height and weight as Rebecca, and she has red hair!'

Detective Mills ran his fingers through his hair, deep in thought. He paced up and down the corridor, thinking about the possibility of it being Erin Reid. She was the only one at home and could have snuck back in later, or even before Rebecca had returned home. What if she'd paid someone to kill her husband and conveniently gone out shopping, so they would see her face on CCTV cameras. He voiced his concerns to Xavier who thought it sounded plausible.

Then Townsend said, 'I've always felt there was a dark side to Erin Reid. She seems to watch from an ivory tower, down at the action. Maybe even like a puppeteer, creating the action from above, looking down.'

Mills peered at him with his eyebrows raised, 'Actually, that's quite a good analogy of Mrs Reid. What about Molly's murder, I think Rebecca said she was at home with her mother. Erin said she went to bed early, but she could have snuck out. And with Mrs Rook's murder, she could easily have done it. Nobody was monitoring anything.'

Townsend said, 'When you put it like that, it could all make sense, whenever anyone gets close to Rebecca, they get hurt. The only thing we need to do now is get clarification from the CCTV Forensics Unit. As soon as we have confirmation of that, we'll have our man!' He smiled at Detective Mills.

Mills was smiling too, 'Or woman, well, one way or the other, we will break them down. It's Erin or Rebecca. God, Xavier, who would have thought it! You know what I'd say after this case?' He looked like a schoolboy about to go on a much-awaited holiday with his friends.

'What would you say, Chief?'

'I'd say, never mess with redheads, they could be the death of you!'

'A bit late for that, Chief, my missus is a redhead!'

Detective Mills laughed, 'Yeah, it's too late for you. I'd watch your back if I were you! Now, let's sort this mess out. We need to get forensics to get a wiggle on.'

'Yes boss.'

'Ok, we'll go in – not a word from you. I'll handle it, ok, Xavier?'

'Sure thing.'

Back in the interview room, Rebecca had controlled herself and stopped crying. Detective Mills said, 'Ok, Rebecca, we will let you go for now.'

Townsend stared at him in awe – *what's he doing? If it's her, he's letting her get away, and if it's Erin, she will warn her, and they will be nowhere!*

'Oh, thanks, Detective,' she said, blowing her nose. 'I told you it wasn't me. Did you see the picture clearly and figure it was someone else?'

'Yes, we got a good look, and it was a random woman, or it could have been a man with a wig. There is no doubt at all. You must stay in town, until this is wrapped up. We need your full co-operation. Is that ok?'

'Of course. I want to go home now, it's been a terrible day.'

Mills looked at Townsend, 'Can you take Rebecca to the ladies first, she may need to freshen up, then escort her out. After that, meet me in my office.'

'Yes sir.' He tried to sound normal, but he was perplexed. He was sure that Detective Mills was experienced and smart. There was no way he would just let her go – he must have a plan.

17

When Erin Reid got home, she paced her living room floor, deep in thought. Nothing was right, everything was wrong, and she felt it. Rebecca was her only priority as far as she was concerned. Nobody else mattered and she would do anything and everything in her power to protect her.

She told the female police officer she should go, but then she said, she was under orders to only leave when her daughter or Frank returned. Erin didn't want anyone monitoring her, she liked her space.

Erin thought about everything and knew the end was nigh, the whole truth would come out, and she had to tell Rebecca before she found out from someone else or even worse, the police!

After a while, there was the knock on the front door. She opened it to find Frank, 'Hey you, come in. Where is that police officer?'

'Hi Erin, she claimed she was allowed to leave if either Rebecca or I turned up, so she's gone.'

Once Frank was inside, Erin closed the door. 'I don't want anybody following me, it makes me claustrophobic.'

'You both need monitoring, with a killer on the loose targeting the two of you. Who knows, I'm a target now too.'

Erin stared at him apologetically, 'Sorry, yes you are. Poor thing.'

He smiled, 'Don't worry, I can look after myself.'

She turned her back to him, 'I know you can. You are very special to Rebecca.'

'Aw, Erin, I hope so. I love her so much, I haven't told her, but I do.'

She put the kettle on, turned back and giving him a smile, she said, 'Yes, I suspected, I've known for a long time, Frank. So, did they give you a rough time?'

'The detectives?'

She nodded.

'Oh, not really, I put them in their place. They've got nothing on me. I didn't kill anyone, so I'm not bothered. I want Rebecca to come back, I hope they aren't giving her grief.'

'Why did you come back here, Frank?'

'Rebecca asked me to. She was worried because you were alone. I didn't know they'd ordered the police officer to wait till someone else got here. If I'd known that, I would have waited for her.'

'Oh, ok.'

'I told Frey to call me as soon as she's done, I don't want her coming back alone with a killer targeting her!'

'Yes, pick her up from the station when she has finished, I'll stay here.'

'I can't leave you alone, no, you have to come with me when she calls.'

'Frank please, I will lock up carefully and close the doors behind you. I need to go to bed and not be disturbed, I'm exhausted, I didn't sleep well last night again.'

'You do look tired now, why don't you sit down, and I'll make us tea… or coffee. What would you prefer?'

'Whatever you're having.'

Frank made them some tea and a sandwich, he was starving, Erin hadn't eaten either. They both ate in silence for a while, then Frank said, 'Whilst I was at the station I realised everything that has happened has revolved around Rebecca. At first, the detectives suspected it was Matt and Rebecca because both his mum and Molly died in the same suspicious circumstances, but now that Matt has gone, it can only be Rebecca. She's the one at the centre of it all. Don't you think, Erin?'

Whilst he was talking, Erin looked like she had gone into a trance. She was silent, her face frozen as if she had seen a ghost.

'Erin, are you ok?'

She snapped out of her daze, 'Sorry, yes you are right, it's Rebecca that this whole thing is centred around.'

'Guess what my uncle suggested? He said both of you should come to Scotland for a month till the police find the monster who's setting about killing everyone around Rebecca.'

Erin's eyes widened, 'I don't want to go back there.' She said a tad too loudly.

'Why not?' Frank could tell he touched a nerve.

In an effort to shift focus from her fears she said, 'Oh, that's a good idea, but I don't want to go, and I don't think Rebecca would like that idea either. She likes the comfort of her own home.'

'Yeah, but there will be no comfort if someone kills either one of you, will there? Please, Erin, consider it from a safety point of view. It's more for that than anything. Right now, my uncle is worried about me too.'

'Oh no, of course he would be.'

'I called him today after I left the station, and he was practically in tears. He said, what if what happened to Matt happened to me? He knows I can protect myself, one-on-one, but if they stunned or drugged me and set the place on fire, that would be it.'

Erin looked shocked. Frank continued, 'When I see it from his perspective I am scared, of course. If we all go to Scotland, then we will be so much safer than here. Please, will you think about it? That way, my uncle will get some peace of mind too,' he begged.

She watched him talk, thinking how lucky Rebecca was to have not only a man as handsome as Frank in love with her, but also to have someone so devoted to her. It was really nice. They made a great couple – she would definitely approve if Frank asked her Rebecca to marry him. She smiled at the thought.

'What are you smiling at?'

'Oh nothing, just a private joke, really.'

Just then, Frank's phone rang, he'd left it in the kitchen and rushed over to get it before it rung off, saying, 'About time too! It must be Rebecca saying she's ready to leave.'

But when he looked at it he was confused. It was an unfamiliar number. He picked it up, wondering who it could be, 'Hello?'

'Frank, it's me, can you pick me up?'

'Yes, sure I can, where are you, at the station?'

'I'm not sure. The police were really rude but finally let me go, so I left the station and just walked, and now I'm kind of lost.'

'God, Frey, it is dangerous, why the hell did you do that? I told you to ring me, and I'd pick you up from the station.'

'I couldn't think, I was upset.'

'Frey, have you been drinking? You sound strange, are you ok?'

'Yes, I'm fine. Please, can you come quickly, I'm scared.'

Erin had now joined Frank in the kitchen and was standing next to him, her eyes had clouded over, and her brow furrowed in worry.

'Whose phone is this, it says unknown number?'

'I'm at a payphone, I lost my phone. It was in my hand when I left the station, but now it's gone, I don't know if I dropped it somewhere. I was so upset Frank, please come quickly. And bring Mother, I don't want her left alone at home for that killer to get her.'

'Yeah, ok, I'm coming. Can you tell me where you are? You must be near the station, right?'

'I'm not sure, I walked for a while and then jumped on a bus, thinking it was going towards home, but it wasn't so I got off. Now I don't know where I am. Hang on a minute.'

He heard silence. Erin asked, 'What's happening?'

'She says she's lost somewhere. She couldn't think straight, so she left the station walking and…'

'Frank, are you there?'

'Yes, I am.'

'I'll call you in a second. Let me get the full address from someone local.'

She rang off before he could respond. Erin looked at him, 'She said she will ring as soon as she finds an address she can give me. She doesn't sound right. I can't believe the police allowed her to go like that. God, I wish I'd stayed back now.'

Erin was shaking, so she sat on the breakfast bar stool.

His phone rang again from the unknown number, he picked it up, 'Frank have you got a pen?'

'Yes, just tell me,' he barked. None of this would have happened if she'd stayed at the station.

'358 Colville Road. It's in Beckenham.'

'I know that area, there are warehouses around

there. What are you doing there, Frey? That's like five or six miles away from the station.'

'I told you, I took a bus, come soon please, I'm cold.'

'Ok, see you soon, and don't stand on the road, go to the back of a building or something so that nobody can see you.'

'Yeah, good idea, I will. Come quickly.'

'I'll drive as fast as the road lets me. Frey, don't talk to strangers.'

'I won't,' she laughed and put the phone down.

He glanced at Erin, 'Don't worry, we will get her. She sounded scared but was laughing too. She must have loosened up. Come on, let's hurry.'

They both rushed out of the house and jumped into Frank's car, he tried to relax, but it was hard trying not to drive too fast. It was already four in the afternoon, and in an hour or two, it would be getting dark. He wanted to have them back home before then, he didn't like the thought of them being out in the dark. Erin sat quietly beside him, looking out of the window. She clasped both her palms together and was twisting and turning her hands repeatedly. He could see she was agitated.

He knew the way, but he couldn't understand what she was doing there. What if she'd lost her mind and was just wandering around not knowing who or where she was? Frank played out every possibility in his mind.

He couldn't stand the silence anymore, so he said,

'She sounded weird. Not herself, do you think she's losing it over all this?'

Erin said nothing for a while, Frank was worried about her too. Then she said, 'I'm not sure, maybe Matt's death is sinking in. I thought she was taking it quite well earlier.'

'Yeah, I didn't think of it from that angle. It could be because of Matt's death. Or there may be another reason too Erin, she may have been manhandled by the police. She must have been through the wringer. I know I felt pretty drained the first time they talked to me. They really gave me a hard time. Today, it was easier.'

Erin went quiet again. He let her stay with her thoughts. He drove the rest of the way in silence. It took about half an hour to get to the warehouse. It looked deserted. Frank parked up and shouted, 'Rebecca! Can you hear me?'

There was no response. Erin was now out of the car, too. They looked around the area. There were several warehouses, but all of them looked either abandoned or empty. They walked along till they found the number of the warehouse Rebecca said she was waiting in, Frank said, 'Erin, here is number 358.' He shouted again, 'Rebecca!'

But there was no answer, Erin also called out her name in panic, but the place was silent. Frank said, 'What if someone got to her, or she's injured and lying on the floor somewhere inside?'

Erin said, 'Yes, she could have passed out – you did say she sounded peculiar.'

Just then, they heard a noise from the back of the building, they both ran towards it. At the side of the property was a set of metal stairs. A woman was standing at the top and shouted, 'Are you Rebecca's mum and Frank?'

Frank answered, 'Yes we are, is Rebecca inside, and is she ok?'

'Yes, she is, hurry, she says she's not feeling well.'

Frank ran up at lightning speed, and Erin followed as fast as she could. The woman was young and pretty with a mass of brown hair and dark glasses. He found it odd to see a woman here, alone with Rebecca, but all he could think about was trying to get to her as quickly as possible.

At the top of the stairs, he asked, 'God, where is she?'

'In there, hurry!' she said, pointing at the metal door in front of him.

He ran inside, and the woman followed him. He searched around for Rebecca, the whole area looked dusty, dark and had unpainted walls.

A moment later he said, 'Ouch that hurts.' He felt himself falling, then blacked out.

18

Rebecca walked into the toilet and gave her face a good wash. She was glad the detective suggested she freshen up. How could she meet Frank looking like this? After she'd done the best she could to cool her puffy eyes, she wet her hair, fiddling with it till she got it to sit right.

When she left the restroom, she called Frank, but there was no answer. It was four-thirty in the afternoon; he'd said he'd pick her up when she was ready. She tried him again several times, but his phone was going straight to voicemail.

Feeling annoyed, she decided to take a taxi back home. She wished she'd driven herself there, but she'd been a mess that morning and in no fit state to drive after finding out about the fire. She walked over to the receptionist and asked, 'Miss, have you got a number for a taxi, or can someone from the police drive me home?'

The blonde lady at the desk didn't look amused. She stretched over, grabbed a piece of paper and shoved it into Rebecca's hand. 'Here's a list of taxi drivers, take your pick! We don't provide a taxi service at the police station!' She had a hard, stern look on her face.

Rebecca thanked her and returned to the seating area to call a taxi. She dialled the first few numbers on the list she'd been given, but they either didn't pick up, the wait was over an hour or they didn't service her home location. She wondered when taxi drivers had become so picky!

There were ten numbers on the list, and when she reached number five, the operator said there was an available taxi that could come within five to ten minutes. And then, at last she got a text message from Frank.

'Hey, can you come to this warehouse – 358 Colville Road, in Beckenham? Your mother and I got talking about my ideas for a new office space, and I've found the perfect one. I want you to see it ASAP or I might lose it to another buyer.'

'What?' she said out loud. She sent a message back to him, quickly.

'Have you gone mad? I am tired, and I want to go home. You promised to pick me up! Where is my mum?'

Rebecca waited for a minute then got a message back from him.

'She is here with me too, she is excited about it. Please come soon, we will be here five minutes tops, I'll even pay for the taxi if you want and drive you both home – plus dinner is on me.'

He sent a winking emoji after his message. It confused her, but Frank had never disappointed her before. She was happy he was excited about getting a new office for them. This was the first time she'd heard it mentioned. With a deep sigh, she replied.

'Fine ok, I should be there in fifteen minutes. You owe me big time.'

Rebecca sent her message and put an 'eyes to heaven' emoji. She rang the taxi company to tell them her destination had changed. They said it wasn't a problem. She had to give the new destination to the driver when he came to pick her up.

With the texting and confusion in her head, she didn't hear the taxi sound his horn outside the station. The receptionist shouted over, 'Miss, your carriage awaits outside!'

Rebecca looked over at her, stood up to get her taxi, 'What a nasty woman!' She whispered.

The taxi driver was a nice old man who came out of the car to open the back door for her like a limousine chauffeur. 'Thank you, mister, you're an old-school gentleman. There aren't many taxis that offer such a service.' She got in and buckled herself in as she spoke.

The old man shut the door for her and got in. He laughed, 'Miss, I've been doing this job for over twenty years, and I get rude customers that I hope I'll never meet again. But I have learned to be a good judge of character. When I saw you step out of the station, I thought you looked lost, and I felt you needed someone to be nice for a change. Especially if you've just come out of jail!'

He sat back into his driver's seat and pulled away. Rebecca exclaimed, 'I didn't come out of jail! I went in voluntarily!'

She heard a big belly laugh from the old man, and she knew then that he was teasing her. She smiled too.

'So, you're a taxi driver *and* a comedian. Thank you for making me smile, it's been a dreadful few hours, to be honest. A terrible few months, in fact!'

'Sorry about that, miss,' he said, and then went quiet. After a few minutes, and to break the silence, she talked about the weather, and then the fire that had been in the news, and told the driver that the man killed in the fire was her ex-fiancé. He was shocked and then understood why she had been at the station.

'Don't worry miss, they'll catch the bastard and hang him by his danglies! You stay calm, love.'

She smiled at the expression '*hang him by the danglies*', but her mind wandered to Matt and their time together. It had been good when it started, they'd had many laughs, and memories they created together were still precious to her. The realisation she would never see his face again made her sad. She cared about him, even though she had stopped loving him.

'Here we are, love,' said the driver loudly.

'Great, thank you. I was miles away,' she hurriedly explained.

'I know miss, that's why I stopped talking. For such a young and beautiful girl, you have tons on your plate. Now then, what do you want to do here? There's nobody about, and I don't want you to come to any harm if you are left alone.' The old man scanned the area as he spoke to her.

'Oh no, I won't be alone. Can you see that silver BMW over there?' she said, pointing at Frank's car.

'Yup.'

'That's my boss's car, and he wants to move our offices here. So, he wanted me to check it out to see if was suitable.'

Her explanation satisfied him, so after paying her fare, she got out and waved him off. He called after her, 'Are you sure you don't want me to wait for you?'

She yelled back, 'No, thank you, safe driving.'

He smiled at her and drove off.

Rebecca walked to Frank's car, but noticed he wasn't parked near the warehouse marked 358. She walked towards the warehouse. It was very quiet.

When she got closer to number 358, she still couldn't hear anything. Rebecca shouted, 'Frank? Mum?'

Nothing.

Then her phone notified her she had a message. She fished it out of her bag and looked at it. It was from Frank.

'Are you here yet? When you get here, come to the rear of the building, there are metal stairs. I am inside.'

She knitted her eyebrows in confusion, she walked quickly now she knew where she had to meet him. She climbed up the stairs. Her little black ballerina pumps slipped on the first few rungs, so she gripped onto the railing tightly before she went any further.

When she reached the top, she resisted the urge to knock on the metal door in front of her. Her mum and Frank were inside, and she had permission to go in, so she turned the handle and stepped inside.

It was darker than the outside. The sun was setting, so the place looked dingy, the room was an immense space, sixty square feet and had only two windows that didn't allow much light in. The walls were bare concrete, the large room looked dusty, and the air smelt stale and damp. She shouted, 'Mum? Frank?'

She heard grunting in the far corner of the room. She peered at where the noise was coming from, but she couldn't see properly, so she got her phone out to put the flashlight on. But as she searched in her bag, she felt something cold and sharp at the back of her neck and a woman said, 'Don't fucking move. Drop the bag and phone!'

~

Detective Chief Inspector Christopher Mills and Detective Sargent Xavier Townsend reconvened in their office after Rebecca had left.

Xavier couldn't wait to find out why Chris had sent Rebecca home. He asked, 'Chief, what's the deal? I thought we'd narrowed the suspects to either Rebecca or Erin!'

'Slow down Xavier, whilst you took Rebecca to get freshened up, I made a call to Boris to find out if he'd got any closer to finding out who that person was. He said they were still working on it, so I contacted our boys on the ground to get them to follow Rebecca. Didn't she say she was waiting for Frank Pearson to pick her up?'

'Yes, I think so, why, do you want her followed?'

'Until we get something concrete from our forensic boys, I want them to assume everything is ok. I need her to tell her mum about the questions we asked her so that Mrs Reid will know we are close. If either of them did it, and they suspect we are onto them, they will make a mistake, and soon, I am sure. So, getting them followed will uncover answers. Now, let's watch the fun!'

There was a knock on the door, it was Chief Constable Ryan, 'Chief we've got an issue. Rebecca waited at the reception for a while then went home in a taxi. Shall we still wait for Mr Pearson and follow him then?'

Mills stared at him him in disbelief. His eyes narrowed, and he tried to keep his temper in check, 'For God's sake Ryan, I told you to follow her wherever she went! Why didn't you follow the taxi?'

He looked at both men, frowning, 'You said follow Frank when he collected Rebecca, we didn't realise you wanted a tail on her we thought it was Frank! I'm sorry, boss.'

Mills shouted, 'Get to her home, ASAP! I need to know what they're up to at all times, and whilst you're on the way, find out from the taxi companies if she went straight home or to Frank Pearson's house, or you will need to make another trip sharpish! Mr Pearson's life could be in danger!'

Ryan's face flushed, 'Yes, Chief. We will rush there now.'

Townsend was now worried for Frank's life too, 'Ryan you concentrate on getting to Miss Reid's house, and I will call the taxi firm. If I find out she has gone somewhere else, I will let you know, so listen out for your radio and phone, ok?'

'Yes, sir.'

When he left, both the detectives rushed to get the taxi number from Margaret, the blonde receptionist. 'I gave her this list,' she said, handing the sheet of paper with the taxi numbers printed on it.

Mills asked, 'So which one did she call?'

'I would guess the first on the list, but I'm not sure.'

Townsend was losing his patience with Margaret, 'God's sake, she's as useful as a chocolate teapot!' he muttered. Looking at Mills, he said, 'Come on boss, you ring the first one, I'll ring the second, and we keep going until we get to the taxi company that picked her up.'

They rang the various companies. When they finally got to the taxi company that Rebecca had used, they were told she'd ordered a taxi to take her home. Satisfied that Constable Ryan would be there soon, they waited for his call.

After a tense fifteen minutes and a cup of coffee each, drunk by both detectives to calm their nerves, they got the call they were waiting for. Detective Mills picked up the phone on the first ring.

'Chief it's Ryan here, the house is empty, sir. Both the ladies' cars are here, but nobody's in. We knocked, on the pretence of checking Rebecca got home ok, so they wouldn't suspect what we were up to, but nobody answered.'

'What? Did you try to peer through the windows, go to the back of the house? Check for sounds or if any lights were on inside?'

'Yes, Chief, we did all that. I don't think she took the taxi here, sir.' Ryan quietened his voice as he spoke.

Mills kept himself in check, he knew he was intimidating Ryan, 'Ok, good job, Ryan. Can you go to Frank Pearson's apartment please? I presume you have his address?'

'Yes sir, we'll go there right away.'

Mills put the phone down and said to Xavier, 'She isn't there.'

'I gathered that. I guess we should call Frank and check that he's ok and whether Rebecca is with him before Ryan gets there.'

'Good idea, I'll make out I need to ask him some routine questions I missed. Then I'll check whether Rebecca got home. He can tell me if she's there or not, or even if Mrs Reid is there with him. You contact that taxi company and get them to confirm exactly where they took Rebecca. And Xavier?'

'Yes, Chief?'

'Tell them the driver didn't take her home, insist on an exact address. Maybe she said home, but when the driver picked her up, she changed her mind. And try to speak to the actual driver that picked her up. I want to know what happened in that taxi after she left here.'

'I'm on it.'

As they were trying to work out where Rebecca had gone, Detective Mills was hitting a brick wall trying to get Frank Pearson on the phone. His calls were diverting straight to voicemail. After the third attempt, he left a message for Frank to call him back as soon as possible. Mills told him he'd had an important breakthrough in the case – he hoped that would entice Frank to call back quickly.

He noticed Detective Townsend was also having a frustrating time with the taxi company. He put down the phone, 'Bloody hell, they're the dumbest people I know! The silly woman on the phone said she only recorded the first address, Rebecca's home address. She said Rebecca called again to change her destination, but the operator didn't note it down. She told Rebecca to give the change of destination to the driver.' He rubbed his forehead, he could feel another headache coming on.

Mills asked, 'So now what?'

'I told them it was a matter of life and death, that they urgently needed to talk to the driver who picked up Rebecca and to call me back with the details. She said they keep records of all their drivers' contact numbers. She's going to try to get hold of him and call me back.'

'Good, how long did she say she'll take?'

'Five minutes she said, but let's see.'

After a few minutes and some frantic pacing from both the detectives, looking at their phones for messages or calls, Townsend's phone rang. He nodded when he heard the person at the other end of the line and took down notes. He said, 'Yes, ok I got that. I will ring him if I need more information, so tell him to keep his phone free.' He thanked the operator for her fast response and ended the call.

'Got it, Chief. 358 Colville Road. It's in Beckenham.'

'Thank God, let's go,' said Mills.

19

Rebecca dropped her bag with her phone inside immediately she was asked to do so. She could tell that the woman meant business. At last she would find out, one way or the other, who was behind making her life a misery.

'Walk forward bitch!'

Rebecca did as she was told. She walked ahead, scanning the warehouse for her mother and Frank. She heard grunting in the corner of the room and she looked in that direction again. Her eyes had now become accustomed to the darkness, and she could make out two figures in the corner. One was sitting on a chair and the other standing by a pillar.

She yelled, 'Mum, Frank is that you?'

From what she could gather, her mum was on the chair, she grunted and nodded.

Rebecca was now terrified, 'Oh my God, what have you done to her?'

The woman's cold voice answered back, 'Nothing she doesn't deserve. Now, come along, my beautiful Rebecca. I reserved a nice seat for you over there.'

She pushed Rebecca toward a chair opposite her mum and Frank. In a sing-song voice, she said, 'Please my darling, sit down and tie yourself to the chair, if you don't mind. I have left you some cable ties, and make sure you secure yourself tightly, or I will become angry and trust me, you don't want that!'

Rebecca begged, 'No, please, why are you doing this?' She tried to get a glimpse of the woman, but she only saw her dark hair and her face hidden behind a large pair of sunglasses.

'No, no, no, it's not time yet, my lovely. Just do as I say, or our sexy Frank over there will get more flesh sliced out of him!'

Rebecca moaned, 'Please don't, ok, I will do as you ask.' She knew this woman was serious. She was responsible for all the killings and the fire. The last thing Rebecca wanted was to antagonise her. She had to keep her wits about her and do everything in her power to get them out of there alive.

Walking over to the chair indicated, she sat and tied one of her wrists to one arm of the chair. She couldn't possibly tie herself to the other side. The woman said, 'Relax, I'll do it.'

She kept her head down, came over to Rebecca and grabbed hold of her hand. She placed the knife on the floor and roughly tied Rebecca's free hand to the chair to securely fasten her. Next, she walked to the window sill where she kept more of the cable ties and restrained Rebecca's legs so that she couldn't get free.

Rebecca was less interested in being tied up and more worried about why Frank was so silent and what had happened to her mother.

The woman stood back to admire her work, she said, 'Now then, everything is as it should be.' She wandered over to Erin, removed the gag that was keeping her silent and moved up close to her ear, 'Now shhh, don't make a sound, or our lovely Rebecca will get a shock or two from my stun gun, like Frank over there!'

Erin sobbed, 'Please stop this, we have money if that's what you want. Take everything, please let us go.'

The woman laughed, 'If I'd wanted money, trust me, I'd have had it ages ago. Do you know how many times I have been in your house?' Erin made a whimpering sound. 'Yes, you should be scared, I know all about you and your house, inside and out!' she laughed.

Rebecca asked, 'Mum, what's wrong with Frank?'

Erin stopped crying and said, 'She… she…'

The woman said, 'Go on, Erin dearest, tell her. I'd prefer her to hear it from you.'

Erin tried again, '… she stunned him with that gun, then she tied him to that pillar. Every time he tries to escape, she stuns him again, and I think she's hurt him with the knife. He's unconscious.'

Rebecca's scream cut through the dank, dusty air, 'No! Why are you doing this?'

The woman said, 'Rebecca, calm yourself, I want to tell you a little story.' She turned to Erin and said, 'Now

Mummy, say nothing whilst I explain your dirty little secret to our poor, innocent, lovely Rebecca. If I hear so much as a word, I will give you a little slice with my knife. You got that?'

Erin nodded, terrified. 'Great, now Rebecca, let's start.'

The woman stood in front of Rebecca, took off her sunglasses and pulled off her wig and shook her red hair loose from its restraints. Rebecca stared at her in amazement, she must be going mad. The lady in front of her was identical to her.

'I am your twin sister, Zoe.'

Rebecca opened her mouth and yelled, 'Oh my God, Mum?'

'Now, now,' Zoe said, I told your mum not to speak. Don't worry Beckie, she knows I exist, after all, she gave birth to us! Zoe stole a glimpse at Erin.

'Now, where was I? Oh yes, let me start from the beginning. We were born in a tiny town in Scotland, and we lived like sisters, so I am told. Then one fine day, our mother over there,' she pointed accusingly at Erin, 'decided she didn't want me! Do you know *why*, Beckie?' She screamed the question at Rebecca.

Rebecca who was still stunned, looking at the girl who was her duplicate, shook her head to say she didn't.

'Because I wasn't perfect like you, and we know how our mother loves perfect things! I was a sickly child, I was always tired and sleepy and whilst we were still babies, mother dearest got fed with of me dragging everyone down, so she arranged a convenient little illegal adoption for me.

When we were just tiny toddlers, she gave me to a midwife called Patricia who became my '*so-called*' adoptive mum. Let's just say Patricia wasn't very nice. She didn't feed me properly, she left me alone for most of the day. She was too busy with her career to even enrol me into school on time. So I was six when I started school and got to interact with other children for the first time. Obviously, I found that difficult. I went from being an only child, playing alone, to going to a school and having hundreds of children around me.

'I was off sick a lot, and no one could figure out what was wrong with me. Finally, when I was nine years old, I was diagnosed with Addison's Disease. My teenage years were a disaster, they bullied me because I was weak and harassed at school for being different.

'Then, when I was fourteen, my adoptive mother got a new boyfriend. That bastard decided he liked young girls.'

Rebecca raised her eyebrows, and Zoe said, 'You weren't expecting that, were you, Beckie?'

Rebecca said nothing, Zoe continued, 'When that asshole suggested we do more, you see, he needed my consent to continue, I told my mum about what he wanted, and guess what? She didn't give a shit!' Her voice rose to a shrill screech.

Zoe turned her back to Rebecca and continued, 'This cat-and-mouse game with him continued till I was sixteen years old. So, for two years I had to endure his advances. And because he was more interested in me than her, she beat me every day. She was clever, she ensured my bruises weren't on my arms, legs or face. Sometimes I couldn't move for days because of her constant physical abuse — usually during school holidays. She hurt me the most then, she knew I didn't have to go to school so my body would recover before I had to go out! Patricia suspected he was only with her because he wanted to get me into bed, and she hated me for that. She hit me because I was sickly and because her boyfriend wanted me more than he did her!

'Now, as you can see, I didn't have an easy life. Patricia finally chucked him out when she woke up one night to find he wasn't in bed with her. She came into my bedroom and found him raping me. He had his hand over my mouth whilst trying to undress me. She got the rolling pin and hit him hard on the back of his neck and continued to beat him while I crawled to the other side of my bed. He was screaming in pain and I in fright.

'But she never killed him. When he came round, she told him to get out or she would report the incident. She never talked to me ever again after that. I think she blamed me for his what he did. Don't forget Beckie, like you, I was coming of age, growing into a woman and getting more attractive. After that nasty incident, she pretty much left me alone, she didn't talk to me much, and I preferred it that way.

When I turned twenty and was about to leave that horrible bitch, my '*mother*' — Erin over there adopted me to — we had a massive fight. She refused to let me leave, she barred the front door to prevent me from going, so I punched her away. The stupid cow lost her balance and hit her head on the edge of the side table and slumped to the floor! There was blood everywhere. I didn't bother helping her.' Zoe said, smiling, reliving the incident.

Rebecca still said nothing. Zoe went on, 'So you see, my darling girl, I could have saved her, but I didn't want to. I enjoyed seeing her die, I watched her life ebb away from her and when I didn't think anyone could save her, I called the ambulance. They said she'd died minutes before they got there. You don't know how happy I was. That was when I got a taste for it — killing. It wasn't hard to do. Especially when you can get people to believe it was an accident!

'It was when I was sorting through Patricia's papers after her death that I got the surprise of my life. I found out, *Lo-and-behold*,' Zoe raised her hands theatrically.

'I didn't belong to her! I was a twin! I didn't know whether to laugh or cry. In her journals, she explained that my real mum, the bitch,' she pointed her knife over to Erin, 'didn't want me because I was always poorly. She gave me up and moved to London with you and that spineless father of ours who didn't have the balls to defend me!'

Rebecca was still scared and shocked to speak, so she said nothing, she was trying hard to make sense of everything that Zoe was telling her.

Suddenly, Zoe became agitated and roared, 'Do you know how that made me *feel*? To find out I would have lived a happy life with you as my sister and a loving family's arms around me? It was because of my Addison's Disease, that's why Erin didn't want me, that's why she persuaded Finn to give me away. The more I spied on our family, the more heartbroken I became.'

Shaking her head and crying, Rebecca said a quiet voice, 'I can't even imagine it!'

'Well, at least you are honest, my darling Beckie. Not like that bitch of a mother of ours!' Zoe kneeled beside Rebecca and said, 'I wanted to die Beckie, I couldn't believe I'd been treated like dirt by everyone. If you'd found out the truth, we could have been sisters.' Zoe cried.

'Then why didn't you come to talk to me Zoe, why did you have to kill all those people? We could have sorted it out. Our dad was a nice man.'

Zoe got up in a shot and screamed, 'Enough! I don't want you to defend them. Don't be a fool my darling Beckie. Don't become like them! Weak and stupid!'

Just then, Frank moaned as he regained consciousness. Zoe turned around quickly to check on him.

Rebecca said, 'Frank, it's me, Rebecca. Wake up.'

Frank opened his eyes and scanned the room. The first thing he saw was his Frey. He smiled and said, 'Oh my God Frey, you are a sight for sore eyes. There is a mad woman around who tied your mum up and stunned me with her gun. Untie me quickly before she gets back.' Every word he said was a struggle. He heard Erin crying and someone else say, 'Frank, I'm over here.'

Zoe smiled at him and said, 'I am beautiful, aren't I? Just like your lovely Frey!'

It confused him, what was she trying to tell him? His whole body hurt. His head felt as if someone had kicked it like a football. His speech was slurred, 'Hurry… untie me, Frey. That woman will be back… hurry. I am losing my energy.'

From somewhere in the back someone said, 'Don't talk to her Frank, I'm here.'

Frank tried looking over Zoe's shoulder, to make out who was talking to him, but he was so confused. Zoe said, 'My, my, aren't you a handsome young man? My Beckie chose well. I didn't much like that bastard, Matt! I hated him, I wanted to kill him long before the fire – I wanted him to go first actually, but I thought I would make them all wait and see the fun I could unleash!' She laughed at her joke.

Whilst she talked, Frank's legs buckled. He couldn't hear what Rebecca was saying. He spoke in a low rasping voice, 'Rebecca, did you kill Matt and all the others? Please, darling, don't tell me you did. I love you, how can I help you if you did that?'

Erin spoke, she didn't care. She didn't want Frank for even one moment to think her Rebecca could do such a thing, 'Frank don't believe this woman. Rebecca didn't do that. This is her twin, Zoe!'

Zoe marched over to Erin and bawled, 'Shut up you bitch!' and slapped her hard across the face. From the other side of the room, Rebecca screamed, 'No! Please don't hurt her!'

Frank stretched to see beyond the two women and managed to make out another woman sitting on a chair opposite him, about ten to fifteen feet away. 'Frey?'

Despite the slap, and before she received another, Erin blurted, 'I am so glad I gave you away. You were sickly and a pain to deal with. Even when you were small, you were always so needy, you never slept at night and you were a constantly crying. If we'd kept you, I would have had a mental breakdown! Now, looking at how you turned out, I am glad I got rid of you!'

Rebecca screamed, 'Mum, don't, she will kill you!'

Turning to Rebecca, Zoe said, 'Beckie, great minds, eh?'

Rebecca screamed as Zoe grabbed the knife from the floor and walked over to Erin.

This time, Frank screamed too, 'No! Please don't. No!'

But with a smile on her face, Zoe drove the knife straight into Erin's abdomen. Erin stared straight into Zoe's eyes then Zoe stabbed her again and again. This was something she'd wanted to do for a long time. Twenty-six years of humiliation and pain and frustration that this woman had put her through, now vented in a matter of seconds.

Erin gasped, 'Rebecca, I love you, forgive me,' before she slumped forward and collapsed. Rebecca screamed, and Zoe walked to Frank.

'One down, one more to go! That way, I'll have Beckie all to myself. What do you say, stud?'

Frank was speechless, he didn't know what was going on anymore. Rebecca could see the knife in Zoe's hand. But just as she was about to stab Frank, all hell broke loose.

The room was suddenly swarming with police. One of them shone a torch straight at Frank and Zoe, whilst others trained their guns on them. A voice called out, 'Put the knife down Rebecca, you do not need to do that.' Detective Chief Inspector Mills was trying to talk her down.

Zoe laughed, 'Oh but I do. I don't want her to be happy! I want her to be sad. Then she will get a taste of what I've been through.'

Mills stole a quick glimpse at Townsend who shook his head, they were both confused but Mill persisted, 'Rebecca, you said you loved Frank, so why would you want to hurt him?'

No one spotted Rebecca, strapped opposite Zoe and Frank in her chair, until she screamed, 'Detectives, get her away from Frank, she's going to kill him, and I think she's killed my mum, too!'

Everyone was distracted by Rebecca's voice and turned away from Zoe to look at Rebecca. It was at that moment they heard Frank's animalistic scream as Zoe's knife plunged into him. There was no stopping the police, then one of them shot Zoe straight in the leg.

It was Zoe's turn to scream as she fell, the knife dropping to her side. A few police officers ran to apprehend Zoe, while the others began cutting Rebecca, Frank and Erin out of their restraints.

'I'm ok, save my mum and Frank. Zoe's just stabbed them! Please, please save them,' Rebecca cried.

Zoe was injured but conscious as the handcuffs went on. She laughed, 'They're dead, Beckie, they're gone now, all we have is each other!'

20

It was a bright and sunny morning. When Rebecca awoke, she looked around in surprise. She wasn't in her own bedroom, this room had light blue walls, a nice comfortable single bed and flowers opposite her, at the foot of her bed, placed on one of those strange tables that hospitals use to serve food to patients.

She sat up, but her neck hurt, and she heard someone say in a quiet, calm voice, 'Bec, you're awake, love. Thank God, I thought you were going to be asleep forever!'

Rebecca looked over, it was Puja. She smiled. 'Where am I?'

Puja spoke to her as if she was a child, 'You are fine, don't worry, but you're in hospital.'

'Hospital! Why?' she asked, trying to sit up, but her neck and head hurt immediately.

'Don't get up so quickly Bec, do you remember anything about yesterday?' Puja stared at her.

'Remember? No, what happened?'

'Last night Beck, do you recall what happened last night?'

Just as Puja said the last few words her entire world collapsed, and she flopped back on to the pillows. She placed her hands on her face and said through her sobs, 'Zoe.'

Puja cradled her, 'Shh, she can't harm you anymore.'

Rebecca pushed her away, 'And my mum and Frank? Are they ok? Did they survive?'

Now it was Puja's turn to cry, she promised herself that she wouldn't, but she couldn't help herself, 'Rebecca your... your...'

Rebecca cried too and asked again, 'my mum, she died, didn't she?'

Puja nodded her head, and they both hugged each other, sobbing.

They didn't notice the detectives had entered until Mills spoke, 'Miss Khan, can you please leave for a while, we have to question her.'

'No, please let her stay detective, I need her,' said Rebecca. As she clung to Puja, she used her spare hand to wipe her eyes with the bed sheet.

'Ok, fine, she can stay, but please, no interruptions, Miss Khan, or I shall have to ask you to leave.'

Puja nodded.

Detective Sargent Xavier Townsend approached

Rebecca, smiled and asked, 'Are you ok, Miss Reid? You've had quite an ordeal.'

Rebecca looked at Townsend, but tears were falling fast from her eyes. He suspected she had learned about her mother.

'Puja told me about my mum!'

'We tried to help her,' he said quietly, coming even closer to her. 'She was alive but died from her wounds before she arrived at the hospital. I'm so sorry.'

She sobbed clutching Puja's hand even tighter. Then Detective Mills spoke. 'I'm very sorry, but we do need to ask you questions about your twin sister, Zoe. Are you ok to answer them?'

She whispered, 'Yes.' And as Mills was about to speak, she asked, 'Nobody told me how Frank is doing! Where is he? He's not…' she trailed off, looking at Puja first and then the detectives.

Puja responded quickly, 'No Bec, he's not dead. But he is in a bad way. They took him into surgery to fix the damage from the stab wounds. He's now in intensive care and they say the next twenty-four hours are crucial. His uncle is with him, so don't worry, he isn't alone.'

Rebecca nodded in relief. Detective Mills knew he had to let Puja answer Rebecca's questions, or he wouldn't get any answers from her. Then he said, 'Can we continue now Rebecca? Will you be ok to answer my questions?'

'Sorry Detective, yes, I'll do my best.'

'Ok, why didn't you tell us you had an identical twin

sister? Did you know about her? Because at no point did you mention her.'

'No, I didn't know I had a twin till she attacked us yesterday. But obviously, my mum knew she existed. It was, and still is, a massive shock. I heard someone shoot out yesterday and they hit Zoe. Is she also…?' She couldn't bring herself to say 'dead'.

Detective Townsend replied, 'No she isn't. She's in a high-security hospital.'

Rebecca could only say, 'Oh.'

Detective Mills asked, 'So, what did she tell you when you got there?'

Rebecca told the detectives and Puja the events of the previous night. She had to stop at the bit about Patricia's boyfriend. Puja cupped her palms over her mouth in horror as Rebecca spoke.

When she had finished, she was exhausted. She asked, 'Have you spoken to her, detectives? Did she tell you any more about the other murders? It was her wasn't it?'

Mills added, 'I am positive it was her, we all are,' he added, looking at Townsend. 'But she's refusing to speak to us.'

'Did you try to talk to her, like is she awake already?'

'Yes, she is, she only has a splintered bone in her leg — it's in a cast. Apart from that, she keeps repeatedly saying she will only talk to you.'

Rebecca widened her eyes in surprise, 'What? I don't want to face her ever again!'

Townsend, who had a soft spot for Rebecca, whispered, 'But Rebecca, we need to close the cases, and without your help, this could drag on forever. If we mike you up and send you over, she will talk to you. That way, we can get everything we require, convict her and send her to prison forever!'

She cried, 'But she killed my parents, and Frank is nearly dead, not to mention the others! How can I face such a monster? And the fact she is my identical twin doesn't help. We are at opposite ends of the spectrum, yet, we look so alike, we shared the same womb! It's unbelievable to even imagine!'

Puja said loudly, 'It's ok Bec, they can't make you do things you don't want! I won't let them!' She came closer to Rebecca and stood next to her in solidarity.

Mills said, 'Miss Kahn is right, and we won't force you to do something you don't wish to, but please, can you think about it? It doesn't have to be now, you could do it in a week if you prefer.'

Rebecca agreed, it was the least she could do. After all, if it hadn't been for the quick thinking and acting of the police, they would all have been killed.

She asked, 'How did you find us in that warehouse, Detectives?'

Townsend smiled and said, 'You've got a new fan, Rebecca. That taxi driver told us. He even called the station today to check if you were ok. He wanted to come and visit you in the hospital, but we told him you weren't up for visitors.'

Rebecca smiled too, 'He was a sweet man. Please

thank him from me if he calls to ask about my welfare, and give him Puja's number, she can schedule a time in which he can come and visit. Is that ok with you, Puja?'

She smiled, 'Of course.'

'Ok, we'd better leave now, we will check on you tomorrow. In case you do change your mind. I'm always optimistic, and if Zoe talks to us, I will let you know.'

Later that day, Logan Pearson visited Rebecca. He told her Frank was still hanging in there, he wanted to find out how she was getting on. Rebecca told him she would be ready to leave tomorrow, although she wished she could stay longer and be close to Frank.

Logan asked, 'I heard you saw Frank earlier, I was on a phone call. He doesn't look good, does he?'

She shook her head and wept again, 'I'm sorry Logan, it's my fault. If he hadn't got involved with me, he wouldn't be in this state now.'

Logan was quick to comfort her, 'Now, now, Rebecca, stop thinking like this. Frank is a law unto himself. He loves you, there is nothing he wouldn't do to help you out. Can't you see how much he loves you? It's always and only ever been you.'

She looked up at him, mopping her eyes, 'I love him as well, I've lost everything I have, I don't think I'd want to live if he went too.'

'He won't, that boy is as resilient as a rubber band. He will spring back in no time. I can't imagine the smile on his face when he hears you say you love him! I am glad you do. I don't think I can go through another few years of him pining for you!' he laughed.

The next day, as Rebecca was getting ready to leave, the detectives came to visit her. They reported that Zoe was still refusing to speak to anyone other than her.

Rebecca walked over to the window. She was thinking about Frank and how strong he was, and how fearless. She knew she had to confront her demons and visit Zoe. If she never saw her again, she would feel like there were still unanswered questions. So, sighing heavily, she turned around and faced the two detectives, 'I will visit her. You're right, I'm the only one who can get the answers we need.'

After deciding with the detectives to meet with Zoe the next day, she went home for the first time since that fatal evening. Everything looked flat and lacklustre. Without her parent's, she didn't even feel like staying there. Luckily for her, Puja said she could live with her for a while. Samuel suggested he come to stay as well, and Rebecca was grateful for her friends.

She didn't sleep well that night. Images she couldn't make sense of filled her dreams. She awoke with a start, she thought she heard a noise but then she realised it was the howling wind outside.

Looking at her watch, she noticed it was six o'clock. It was pointless trying to get back to sleep, so she made herself a coffee and sat at the breakfast bar deep in thought, thinking about everything that had happened. There were a lot of questions she wanted Zoe to answer. The sooner this day was done, the better it would be for everyone.

At nine o'clock, Detectives Mills and Townsend came to pick her up. They took her to the hospital that Zoe had been admitted to. When she arrived, Rebecca was taken to an interview room that had a one-way mirror. She knew she was safe and that they would record her conversation with Zoe.

They brought Zoe through in a wheelchair, her leg in a cast. The hospital worker left the room, leaving the twins alone. Townsend and Mills were looking on from the other side of the mirror. Townsend whispered, 'Unbelievable, I would never be able tell one from the other!'

'Erm… that's why they are called *identical* twins!'

Townsend said, 'Always the joker, aren't you?'

They stopped speaking as Zoe started talking to Rebecca, 'So, my darling Beckie, look at you. I hope you realise you're the most beautiful girl in the world!' she said, laughing.

Rebecca wasn't in the mood for Zoe's madness and asked, 'Why won't you speak to the detectives? What do you want from me?'

Zoe said dismissively, 'Oh those detectives, they won't understand my motives the way you will. I need you to understand why. I want to look at your face when I explain everything to you. For all I know, they wouldn't even have told you anything I said. I only wanted to speak to my sister.' She emphasised the word '*sister*'. 'Wow, do you know how good it is to finally say that? Sister!' she said again.

'Go on, Zoe, tell me why you want to speak with me and only me! Are you going to tell me more about Matt, my dad, Molly and Macy? Did you kill them all?'

'*Our dad*!' screamed Zoe.

Rebecca jumped at being yelled at. Zoe was definitely not of sound mind! Calmly Rebecca said, '*Our dad*, sorry.'

'Yes, I killed them all!' said Zoe, smiling. 'But they aren't the only ones, Beckie, I started before that.'

'What do you mean? You told me about Patricia, there were more?'

'Yes, she was the first bitch I killed. Unfortunately for me, that didn't make me a true killer.'

'What are you talking about?'

'Hitting her head on the table was an accident, I simply didn't call the paramedics in time. That doesn't make me a killer. I got lucky with her. When it came to planning my revenge on our parents, I wanted our mother, Erin, to suffer the most, then our weak-minded dad and last but not the least, you!

So, I planned to kill everyone around you from the least important to the ones closest to you. I worked from the outside of your circle of loved ones so I could slowly but surely get in, to where it hurt you the most, and that meant our parents. And when I got to you, I would decide what I fancied doing.

'Now I like you, Beckie, you didn't cause all the strife they've put me through. But you have been able to enjoy life while I have suffered! I realise you've suffered too, maybe we are equal, well, nearly equal!'

'You're an evil person, how could you do such a thing? Maybe our mother was right, you are sick in the head and she must have seen something horrible in you!' Rebecca cried out.

Zoe leaned forward, and yelled, 'What the fuck are you talking about? She was the evil one, how could she do that to me? Since finding out the truth, haven't you for one moment thought how mother dearest could be so cruel? If I am evil, then I fucking inherited it from her!'

Both the girls were breathing hard, Zoe changed her demeanour. She smiled, 'So don't you want to find out about the others, Beckie? How I worked my way from the outside to the inside?'

Rebecca frowned, 'I am sure you want to gloat about it. So, go on, tell me how evil you've been.'

Zoe's smile broadened, 'So... you want the juicy gossip, eh?'

'Get on with it, Zoe, it's the police that want it, not me!'

'Ok, keep your beautiful hair on, baby girl, so... let's start from the first one. Our gran Rebecca, dear old gran. I suffocated that old hag! I wanted our dad to feel sad, and that was the best way. She didn't die in her sleep. Well, she was asleep when I snuck in and killed her.'

Rebecca's face flushed, she glanced at the mirror so

the detectives could see she wanted to stop hearing any more from her twin sister. Zoe said, 'After that bit of fun, I found out you occasionally met up with Lara, your childhood friend. I never had the chance to have a childhood friend, so I thought I should get rid of her too. That way, we can be equal!'

Rebecca sat upright, she shot forward in her chair and said, 'You evil bitch! She had her whole life in front of her!'

'Yes, she did, but alas! I wanted her out of the way, so I faked a suicide, it wasn't hard for a woman like me Beckie. A typed-up note first, a little bit of chloroform next to make sure she didn't move then a quick injection of heroin – enough to make her overdose – and done! She is dead. I bought my trusty make-up to cover the needle marks. I love what make-up can do, don't you?'

Rebecca spat out, 'You're a sick woman, do you realise that?'

Zoe smiled, 'I don't care Beckie, whatever I am, our mother made me!' She spoke venomously then switched to sweeter tones. 'Then there was poor Macy Rook. Now I took real pleasure in that! You see, I couldn't stand Matt. I don't understand how you stayed with him for so long. I brought his whole house of cards down when I killed Macy!

'The useless police, they blamed it on some senseless mugging! That worked a treat. I had to repeat that murder, so I did with the ugly bitch Molly. Can't you see I was looking out for you? I even sent you that letter.

And I'm so glad I did, you're so predictable, do you know that, Beckie?'

Rebecca said nothing and sat there stunned.

'Why aren't you speaking? I wanted that ugly Molly and Matt to get together but no, he was too hung up on you. I had to send the letter. Then I became fed-up of Molly and whilst I was watching them, opportunity struck.' Zoe laughed.

'God, you should have seen her face. She got out the car quickly to talk to me — obviously she thought it was you she was speaking to. I got talking to her and lured her near that bush and killed her just like I did Macy. And just like that…' Zoe clicked her fingers, '… Molly was dead. It was a wet night, so my tracks were easy to cover. All my plans were going so well Beckie. I'm a pro!'

Even though Rebecca was afraid to ask what happened to her dad, she knew she had to. 'What about our dad? You killed him in cold blood?'

Zoe frowned, 'Of course I killed him. Again, he thought it was you knocking at the door and that you'd forgotten your key. He opened it, he even kissed me on my cheek. He was a weak, spineless man, he listened to Mother too much. If he'd had a backbone, he wouldn't have agreed to everything she said. Coming down to London after getting rid of me. Why did they do that?'

Rebecca shook her head to say she hadn't a clue.

'Because Erin's limited family knew she had twins, she told them she was taking us all to London and wanted to live with her new family alone, so that they wouldn't find out what she'd done. She didn't provide a forwarding address either so that no mail or unwanted guest would make its way to London. Once she agreed to give me away and paid Patricia well to keep quiet, she left with our dad and you to start a new life without me!

'And that useless father of ours agreed. Patricia wrote all about it in her journal. She wrote that the driving force was Erin and only Erin! And because our dad was a coward, he had to die. I knew he had a pace-maker. I've been spying on all of you for ages. Five years of spying gets one a lot of information.

'So, I know everything about you Beckie. Anyway, I bought the stun gun and I gave our father dearest the shock of his life, literally!' She laughed hysterically. 'I planned it all well, then my make-up came out to hide the stun gun marks. It took nearly two minutes to kill him with that gun! I didn't want everyone to be on alert for a killer — I needed to cover my tracks, so I could get everyone on my target list. I wanted you all confused and helpless. And I achieved that didn't I?'

Rebecca screamed, 'No! Please!'

'Well, you needed to find out the truth darling. Did you like that book I left in your room? I thought it was apt – *The History of Scotland*? I needed you to know where you came from, and that you still had close family in Scotland!' She laughed at her own joke and said, 'And guess what? That yappy dog had to go too — the next door's neighbour's '*little*' Lucy. I killed her because she barked every time I came to spy on all of you at night. Your old neighbours don't believe in locking their back door, do they? So, yappy little Lucy was easy!

'I had easy access to your house after our dad died. I made a copy of his keys, I even made a copy of the car keys, in case I needed it in my quest to kill. Those poor foolish detectives, I ran them ragged!' she said, looking toward the mirror.

Rebecca put her palms on her face in disgust, but Zoe continued. She sighed and looked back at Rebecca and said, 'Oh and your Puja. She was another one on my list.'

Rebecca removed her hands from her face and spat, 'Well, you didn't succeed with her.'

Zoe smiled, 'Oh, but I nearly did, I gave her major pain, didn't I? It was touch and go there for a while in the hospital! Imagine my luck in finding out about poor Puja's allergy from none other than you, rambling on that day at the café when you told her you were engaged. I got lucky – I'm great at eaves-dropping!'

Rebecca stood up and yelled, 'That was *you*?'

Sticking her chin out defiantly, Zoe said, 'That was me too, it was so easy to sprinkle those crushed nuts on top of her food. They were so fine, she would never have noticed. And trust me, I used lots! I was unlucky she didn't die, even though I had to put loads on because I figured she'd have her EpiPen nearby. I was so glad she'd left it at home that night, I nearly killed her, stupid bitch. Never mind, I enjoyed watching her suffer and that boyfriend of hers crying like a wimp! What a mess you all were,' she laughed.

Rebecca glared at her, she was speechless. Zoe carried on smiling, 'Then that foolish boy, Matt Rook. God, what did you see in him? You should have seen his face when I knocked on the front door so brazenly. He thought his luck had come in when he saw me. His eyes lit up and everything when I told him I wanted to talk about rekindling our engagement!' Zoe threw her head back and laughed out loud. Then, with a smile still on her face, 'Once I was inside, it was easy. My trusty stun gun, rope and some petrol did the trick. And "*poof*!" up in flames he went!'

Rebecca shouted, 'Oh my God, how could you do that Zoe! None of them did anything to hurt you. I can understand the pain our parents put you through, and if you'd only taken it out on them, it would be understandable but the others? Why, Zoe?'

Zoe shouted, 'Because you had to be miserable like I've been all my life! How could we be alike in so many ways, and you have the good life and me the bad? What did I do wrong, apart from being born with a disease? It was unfair. I needed you to suffer like I've suffered. Eventually, I decided I would never kill you. We would both have to live miserable lives together! I had to do what I did.'

Rebecca whispered, but was still heard by Zoe, 'I still think Mum may have been right. She must have figured out you would be trouble and got rid of you back then!'

'What? You fucking bitch! You're my twin sister. How can you say that! I told you, *she* was the evil one!' screamed Zoe.

'Because it's true. You are a terrible person and have an evil streak in you. Hope you rot in jail forever!' She looked at the mirror and shouted, 'Now please detectives, you've got what you wanted. I never want to see her again. Get me out of here.' Looking back at Zoe, she said, 'I hate you, I never want to look at you again!'

Zoe cried, 'But Beckie, we're the same, we are twins. I know you better than you know yourself. All I have is you. We can try to build a relationship, now I've removed all the rubbish from your life. Please, Beckie, I love you.'

Snarling at her, Rebecca said, 'This isn't love. You destroyed everything because you were selfish and evil! Go burn in hell!'

At that, Rebecca stormed out of the interview room. She could hear Zoe screaming after her, 'Beckie, come back!'

Rebecca ran as fast as her legs could carry her.

After they had dropped her home, Puja said, 'Thank God you're back. How did it go?'

Rebecca shook her head and Puja hugged her, 'Zoe confessed, and we got our outcome, but I can't talk about it yet,' her voice was muffled by Puja's shoulder.

'Darling, you will need counselling. You can't handle this on your own, even with me helping you.'

Rebecca nodded. Puja said, 'The hospital rang.'

'Frank!' thought Rebecca. She pulled away from her

hug, 'God no, don't tell me he… I couldn't handle that too! I need him!' She stared at Puja.

A smiling Puja said, 'No, they said he is out of the danger zone and is asking for you.'

Rebecca smiled but her legs were buckling, 'I need to sit down, or I'll fall over!'

'This is all too much for you. You rest a little, and we will go to the hospital in an hour.'

'No, I've got to visit him straight away, he's stood by me even though his life was in danger. I have to go if he needs me.'

'Ok, ok, relax. Have some tea and a sandwich, then we can go. You're weak. You need to be strong to see him.'

Rebecca did as she said, and within the hour, they were at the hospital. She waited outside Frank's room for Logan to come out and say she could go in alone.

The sight of Frank, lying in the hospital bed looking so weak, made Rebecca want to cry, but Puja had warned her to stay strong, so she tried hard to stifle her tears.

'Hi Frank,' Rebecca whispered as if she would hurt him if she spoke too loud.

He said nothing and stared at her. She got closer, 'It's me, Rebecca.'

He smiled, '*My Frey*?'

It confused Rebecca until she remembered that the last time he'd seen someone like her, it was Zoe. She said, 'Oh, yes, *your Frey*. They've locked Zoe up.'

'Don't talk about her,' he said, closing his eyes in pain.

Rebecca walked swiftly, so she was next to him, 'Frank?'

He opened his eyes and looked at her.

She said, 'I love you, Frank. Never leave me again.'

He smiled, that usual big grin of his. 'Do you how long I've waited for you to say that? I love you so much, Frey. Can we put this all behind us and start again?'

'Yes, please,' she said, smiling at him. 'I would love that so much.' Knowing tears were falling from her face. She didn't care anymore.

EPILOGUE

Detective Chief Inspector Mills was in his office when Detective Sargent Xavier Townsend rushed in, without knocking, a week after Rebecca's meeting with Zoe.

'Chief?'

'Xavier, what a pleasure it is to see you. I thought I told you to go on holiday, so you can come back refreshed for the trial. We need to prepare for court, plus you have loads of leave, what are you doing back in the office?'

'She's killed herself, sir!'

Mills stood up, shocked, 'What? Who?'

'Zoe, sir, she slit her wrists. The nurse found her today. She was long dead!'

Mills furrowed his brow, looking into the far distance, 'Good, I'm glad. If she'd stayed alive, she would have been a thorn in her sister's side. Rebecca would have had to see her in court, and she's been through quite enough. For once, Zoe did the right thing.'

'Yes Chief, I guess she couldn't face life without Rebecca.'

Mills nodded, he was exhausted too.

Townsend asked, 'Shall I make an appointment to meet with Rebecca? She'll need to know before the press gets hold of it.'

'Yes please, and make sure Frank Pearson is with her too. I suspect it will come as a relief to them both.'

Detective Mills slumped back into his chair, mentally exhausted.

A little while later, the detectives met with Rebecca and Frank, who were still at the hospital. Frank was sitting up in bed and Rebecca was reading him a book. Frank looked like he was asleep, but when they entered, he flashed open his eyes.

Detective Mills said, 'Hello Frank, sorry to disturb you from your sleep, we have news.'

'Don't worry detective, I wasn't asleep. Frey was reading, and I was just visualising the story.' He smiled, looking lovingly at Rebecca and then at the detectives.

Rebecca stood up, flinging her hair behind her shoulders and wrinkling her forehead, 'It's about Zoe, isn't it? I can tell!'

'Yes it is Rebecca, we thought we should tell you both as soon as possible,' said Mills.

'What now?' asked Frank, he sounded fed-up and exhausted.

Rebecca said nothing, waiting to hear the detectives' news.

Detective Townsend said, 'Rebecca, you won't have to attend court for Zoe's trial. We have just been informed that she has killed herself. The nurse at the hospital found her this morning. She cut her wrists.'

Rebecca gasped, placed her hands to her mouth and looked at Frank. He opened his arms, and she went to him. She cried, unsure if she was sad she would never see Zoe again or relieved because this terrible chapter in her life was now over.

The pain Zoe had caused would never leave Rebecca, she wondered how two people that were created together could have turned out to be so different. Could her mother have caused it all?

Rebecca closed her eyes in pain as it hit her, like a huge wave finally crashing on the shore. She wailed out loud, 'This was all my mother's doing, she was the one that set those chain of events in motion!

As Frank cradled her in his arms, he knew there was a long road ahead for both of them and hoped that their love — as it had over these last few months, would see them through.

~

ENJOYED GONE TOMORROW?

❧

If you enjoyed this book, I would love for you to leave a review.

Reviews are incredibly valuable to an author. They help spread the word to other readers so they too can discover and enjoy the story.

I thank you for your readership and I hope to bring you many more exciting books in the future.

❧

Don't miss a thing…
Subscribe to my mailing list at:

www.nilzaelita.com

ALSO BY NILZA ELITA

DARE TO IMAGINE: His childhood was based on lies. He found out the truth. Now he wants revenge.

Jonathan has grown up believing he is a normal teenager, but deep down he suspects something is wrong within his family. Desperate to find answers, he gets help from his three extraordinary friends. But what they find out will force him to grow from a teenager into a man in a blink of an eye.

Why did he try to kill himself? Can he persuade his mum to leave his dad before it's too late? Are his friends leading him in the right direction or pursuing their own hidden agenda?

In his quest for the truth, Jonathan must figure out 'the real' from 'the make believe'. Can he wade through a murky swamp of dark secrets, lies and threats without losing his mind, and his life?

If you like surprising plot twists, engaging, thought provoking characters and uncovering human psychology at its worst, then you will love Nilza Elita's captivating novel, Dare to Imagine.

www.nilzaelita.com

ACKNOWLEDGMENTS

Firstly, I would like to thank my family for having the patience with me. They have had to put up with me spending every waking moment on this book, which decreases the amount of time I can spend with them.

I'd like to especially acknowledge my mother, Sidoina, who has taken a big part of that sacrifice by making sure I eat a decent home cooked meal once in a while!

Secondly, I would also like to acknowledge my friends who still remain loyal, even thought I have not spent much time with them. I thank you for sticking by me — you know who you are.

And finally… I would like to thank you the reader. Without you buying and reading this book, there would be no reason for me to write.

❧

ABOUT THE AUTHOR

～

Nilza Elita is an author that is unafraid to push the boundaries to explore the human mind, she likes mixing real life situations with her fictional characters and can bring out empathy and compassion in her readers.

Nilza was born in Bombay, a city now called Mumbai in India, and has lived in several countries giving her a global perspective, ultimately making her the author she is today.

She spent her childhood years in Dar es Salaam in Tanzania, her teenage years in Lagos, Nigeria. Her late teenage and early adulthood was spent in a beautiful little town in the Borders region of Scotland called Jedburgh.

Nilza studied and got a Bachelor Degree in Business Administration from the Herriot Watt University in Edinburgh, Scotland.

In her spare time, she can be found at the gym attending several group fitness classes.

Nilza lives in London England, enjoying the fast-paced excitement of city life.

For more information about her
book launches, behind the scene information
and author news visit:
nilzaelita.com

Nilza Elita Social Media Platforms
Twitter: NilzaUK
Instagram: Nilza Elita Instagram Posts
Facebook: Nilza Elita Facebook Page
Pinterest: Nilza Elitas Pins

facebook.com/Nilza-Elita-189273191926640

instagram.com/nilza.elita

pinterest.com/pinterest.co.uknilzaelita

twitter.com/NilzaUK

16873678R00166

Printed in Great Britain
by Amazon